Ellie lifted her head and looked at him, her eyes enormous in her pale face. "If there is no other way, then I suppose—yes."

Angelo's brows lifted mockingly. "You are graciousness itself."

"If you wanted a more generous reply," she said, "you should have asked a more willing lady."

"On the contrary, Elena," he said softly. "I think you will suit my purpose very well."

He reached for her hand and made to raise it to his lips, but Ellie snatched it back, flushing.

"Perhaps you'd restrict your overtures to those times when we have an audience to convince, my lord?"

D0834197

SARA CRAVEN was born in south Devon, England, and grew up in a house full of books. She worked as a local journalist, covering everything from flower shows to murders, and started writing for Harlequin in 1975. When not writing, she enjoys film, music, theater, cooking and eating in good restaurants. She now lives near her family in Warwickshire. Sara has appeared as a contestant on the former U.K. Channel Four game show *Fifteen to One,* and in 1997 won the title of Television Mastermind of Great Britain. In 2005, she was a member of the Romantic Novelists' team on the U.K. quiz show *University Challenge—the Professionals.*

WIFE IN THE SHADOWS

SARA CRAVEN

~ Aristocrats' Reluctant Brides ~

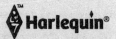

TORONTO NEW YORK LONDON
AMSTERDAM PARIS SYDNEY HAMBURG
STOCKHOLM ATHENS TOKYO MILAN MADRID
PRAGUE WARSAW BUDAPEST AUCKLAND

If you purchased this book without a cover you should be aware
that this book is stolen property. It was reported as "unsold and
destroyed" to the publisher, and neither the author nor the
publisher has received any payment for this "stripped book."

Recycling programs
for this product may
not exist in your area.

ISBN-13: 978-0-373-52830-1

WIFE IN THE SHADOWS

First North American Publication 2011

Copyright © 2011 by Sara Craven

All rights reserved. Except for use in any review, the reproduction or
utilization of this work in whole or in part in any form by any electronic,
mechanical or other means, now known or hereafter invented, including
xerography, photocopying and recording, or in any information storage
or retrieval system, is forbidden without the written permission of the
publisher, Harlequin Enterprises Limited, 225 Duncan Mill Road,
Don Mills, Ontario, Canada M3B 3K9.

This is a work of fiction. Names, characters, places and incidents are
either the product of the author's imagination or are used fictitiously, and
any resemblance to actual persons, living or dead, business establishments,
events or locales is entirely coincidental.

This edition published by arrangement with Harlequin Books S.A.

For questions and comments about the quality of this book
please contact us at Customer_eCare@Harlequin.ca.

® and TM are trademarks of the publisher. Trademarks indicated with
® are registered in the United States Patent and Trademark Office, the
Canadian Trade Marks Office and in other countries.

www.Harlequin.com

Printed in U.S.A.

WIFE IN THE SHADOWS

CHAPTER ONE

April

THE EAR-RINGS WERE the most exquisite she had ever seen.

Nestling in their bed of black velvet, the single diamond drops glowed with a fierce inner fire that made her wonder if her fingertips would burn as she touched them.

But, in fact, they were cold, she thought with a small ironic smile as she fastened them into her earlobes.

Cold as the rest of the jewellery she had been given over the last endless months.

Cold as the chill in the pit of her stomach when she envisaged the evening ahead of her. And its possible aftermath.

She took the pendant, which had been the previous gift, from its case, and handed it to Donata, her maid, to fasten round her throat.

Then she rose from her dressing table, walked to the full-length mirror on an adjacent wall, and stood, straight and silent, subjecting her reflection to a critical, almost clinical examination.

The prescribed outfit for the evening was black, a simple full-length column of silk jersey, long-sleeved, and gathered in soft folds under the bust, its deep neckline revealing the first swell of her breasts, as well as setting off the pendant.

The dress was not in a colour or a style she particularly cared for. It made her look older than her twenty three years, she thought objectively. Conveyed a sophistication she certainly did not possess. But, like so much else in life, it was not her choice.

And, anyway, she asked herself with irony, when had a puppet ever picked its own costume?

Her hair had been swept up into an artfully arranged top-knot, with just a few careless strands allowed to brush her cheeks and the nape of her neck.

She had never really warmed to Donata—the girl was too closely involved in the hollow sham that was her life, and probably saw altogether too much, she thought bitterly—but she could not fault her talent for hairdressing. Or, it seemed, her discretion. Whatever she might think of her employer's marriage, she appeared to keep it to herself.

She had learned to apply her own cosmetics. Practised with shadow, liner and mascara to make the most of the grey-green eyes that were her one real claim to beauty, so that they gleamed almost mysteriously under their fringe of heavily darkened lashes.

Her mouth wore the warm flush of a wild rose, and the same shade was echoed in the polish that enhanced her manicured nails.

And in her ears and at her throat, the diamonds glittered like ice in winter sunlight.

She heard a warning cough from Donata, and saw her glance significantly at her watch.

Time, it seemed, for another performance to begin. Reaching for her evening purse, she walked to the door and out along the gallery to the head of the stairs, hearing from the opposite direction the sound of another door closing.

She paused, as always, watching him walk towards her, tall and lean in the elegance of his evening clothes, and moving as lithely as a panther, as if hinting that the formality of his appearance might only be a façade.

And he halted too, his dark gaze sweeping her in one unhurried, comprehensive assessment.

He gave a swift curt nod indicating that her appearance at least had won his approval, then they began to descend the stairs, side by side, but far enough apart to ensure that not so much as his sleeve would brush her arm.

Then, as they reached the marble floored hall below, she was aware of him turning towards her. She heard his voice say quietly, 'Tonight,' and felt the word shiver across her senses until it became dread.

June the previous year

He had, of course, been ambushed. He realised it as soon as he entered the *salotto* and saw that his grandmother was not as he'd hoped, waiting to receive him alone. Instead, her daughter, Signora Luccino, her plump face set in disapproving lines, was seated beside the Contessa Manzini.

'Dearest Nonna.' He went gracefully to his grandmother's chair, and kissed her slender fingers. 'And Zia Dorotea.' He acknowledged his aunt's presence with a polite inclination of the head that was not quite a bow. 'What a pleasant surprise.'

Well, at least in one respect he was telling the truth, he thought drily. He had certainly not expected to come face to face with his late father's older and least favourite sister, the imposing matriarch who ruled her large family as an absolute despot. But he doubted very much if either of them would derive much pleasure from the encounter.

'*Caro* Angelo.' Cosima Manzini indicated that he should take the sofa opposite. 'You are looking well, dearest.'

He thought he heard his aunt give a quiet snort, but continued to smile pleasantly.

'Thank you, I am in the best of health. Probably more by good fortune than good judgement as I am sure Zia Dorotea wishes to remark.'

'I do not think that riding in a private horse race, when you were still recovering from the shoulder you dislocated in a polo match shows any kind of judgement, my dear Angelo,' said the Signora.

Angelo's smile widened. 'But I had been heavily backed to win—not least by yourself, *zia*, or so my cousin Mauro tells me,' he pointed out softly. 'It would have been most discourteous to let people down, so I did not do so.'

The expression on the Signora's face said plainly that Mauro would suffer for his indiscretion.

'You took a great risk, *caro*,' his grandmother added, her arched brows drawing together.

'A calculated one, Nonna.'

'*Tuttavia*, Angelo *mio*, there is a matter you must now seriously consider.'

His mouth tightened. 'You are again referring, I presume, to marriage.'

'Dear one, I must do.' Cosima leaned forward, her eyes pleading. 'I have no wish to interfere, or to make you angry, but it is over two years since your beloved father died, and you became Count Manzini. You need a son and heir to inherit the title in his turn.'

He said bleakly, 'I am aware of my obligations, Nonna. None better, I assure you. But I do not find them particularly appealing.'

'No,' said his aunt. 'You prefer to trifle with other men's wives rather than find one for yourself. Oh, do not defend him, Mamma,' she added sharply as the Contessa tried to speak. 'It is the truth and Angelo knows it. There are plenty of single girls for him to choose from, but until he stops behaving like a tomcat all over Rome, he will never find a bride.'

He said between his teeth, 'How good of you to take such an interest in my private life, Zia Dorotea.'

'If only it were private,' she retorted. 'But I fear that it is only a matter of time before one of your liaisons becomes a public scandal. And I tell you, Angelo, you will have no-one to blame but yourself if the Galantana brand suffers as a result.'

'We make clothing for the fashion industry, *zia*,' he returned coldly. 'Not church vestments. I hardly think any stories about me as the chairman of the company will affect whether a girl buys a skirt with our label on it or another's.' He shrugged. 'It might even boost sales. Who knows?'

'Oh, you are impossible.' She reached for her bag and rose. 'I have not the patience to reason with you.'

'As I am fast running out of patience to listen to you,' Angelo said crisply. 'Busy yourself with finding a wife for Mauro. That should occupy you for the next several years.'

She gave him a look of concentrated fury and swept to the door. When it had closed behind her, the Contessa said mildly, 'That was neither kind nor polite, *mio caro.*'

'Yet it had the ring of truth she allegedly admires so much. However, I will send her some flowers and make peace.' He was silent for a moment, then sighed irritably. 'She did not come here today, I am sure, just to lecture me on my sins. No doubt she has a suitable candidate in mind as a wife for me.'

'*Davvero*, she mentioned—someone.'

Angelo's face relaxed into faint amusement. 'But of course,' he said softly. 'And are you going to tell me her name?'

'She is called Elena—Helen in her own language.'

'An English girl?' He didn't hide his surprise.

'With Italian blood,' the Contessa nodded. 'Her grandmother Vittoria Silvestre was a dear friend of mine and Dorotea also had affection for her. She married an Englishman, and one of her daughters did the same, a man called Blake. They eventually settled near Genoa, but sadly were killed one winter in an accident on the *autostrada*. Elena, their only child, now lives in Rome, and works as a translator for the Avortino publishing company.'

'She works?' His brows lifted. 'So she is "not just a pretty face" as the English say.'

'You would be a better judge of that than myself.' The Contessa played with her rings. 'It seems you have met her.'

'I have?' Angelo frowned. 'I do not recall.'

She said expressionlessly, 'She was at a dinner party you attended at the house of Silvia Alberoni.' She paused. 'A name that is familiar to you, I think. And certainly a pretty face.'

Under his breath, Angelo cursed his Aunt Dorotea, wondering at the same time how she came by her information.

I shall have to be more careful in future, he thought grimly.

Married to the wealthy but dull head of a firm of top accountants, Silvia was as bored as she was young and beautiful, and also ripe for mischief as he'd swiftly detected at their first meeting. Subsequent and more private encounters had proved her just as ardent and inventive as he'd conjectured, and their *affaire* had prospered.

Until then, he had also believed it to be a secret, which was why he'd risked accepting her invitation to dinner. Most of the other guests had been from the world of finance, so he had found the evening instructive as well as entertaining, but he seemed to remember there had been a girl, quiet and essentially nondescript, seated at the other end of the table. The fact that he'd barely noticed her, he thought, said it all.

He said coolly, 'It is kind of my aunt to bring her to my attention, but I believe I require at least a modicum of personality in the woman I marry. Signora Alberoni's guest seemed—a complete nonentity—a girl without looks or significance.'

'I am sorry to hear it,' his grandmother said after a pause. 'I would not have thought Vittoria's grand-daughter could be so signally lacking in appeal. But any decision must naturally be yours—when you choose to make it.' She paused. 'Now ring the bell, *mio caro*, and Maria will bring coffee.'

And the conversation, to Angelo's relief, turned to other topics.

But that did not mean he was off the hook, he thought, as he drove home later. And in many ways his grandmother and interfering aunt were right. He should be married, and if this might be possible to achieve without having to abandon his bachelor pleasures, he would propose to the first suitable girl who took his eye.

But the experiences of some of his married friends whose submissive doe-eyed brides had turned into control freaks before the honeymoon was over had proved an active deterrent. True, they seemed more philosophical than crushed, but Angelo knew it would not do for him.

But, at the same time, he could not envisage what he might find acceptable either.

He enjoyed women, and the pleasure of women, always making sure that he gave back the delight that he took, but he had never fallen in love with any of the girls who'd shared his bed, or considered that they might also share his future on a long-term basis.

He offered no promises and made it clear he expected none in return.

In addition, there was a kind of inner reserve in him which seemed to warn him when each liaison had run its natural course, and could be safely ended, with charm, generosity— and finality.

And he suspected with a trace of regret that his *affaire* with Silvia Alberoni might already be reaching those limits.

She was a passionate and insatiable mistress, but that reliable antenna of his had recently picked up that she might have begun to foresee a different role in his life for herself, if the worthy Ernesto could be conveniently sidelined.

The word 'annulment' had even been mentioned, lightly and amusingly, it was true, and solely in the context of her failure to become pregnant during the two and a half years of her marriage.

'I was told once that a woman's body can reject the seed of a man she does not truly love.' One crimson-tipped finger had drawn an enticing pattern in the curling dark hair on his chest. 'Do you think that is true, *mi amore*?'

He had curbed his instinct to dismiss the idea as ludicrous nonsense but in much pithier terms, and, instead, murmured some meaningless platitude about a woman's sensitivity which appeared to satisfy her. But the exchange had raised a red flag in his consciousness just the same. As did her use of the word 'love' which he'd always deliberately avoided in his *affaires*.

But even more alarming was the possibility that rumours might be circulating about them. That if Zia Dorotea had learned of their relationship, then others might also have done so, and that the stories might eventually reach Ernesto Alberoni.

Angelo would deny them, of course, but he had to ask himself if Silvia could be trusted to do the same, or if she might see this as an opportunity to escape from a disappointing marriage, and find a husband more to her taste. And there was a real danger she might want it to be him. Could insist that having destroyed her marriage, he had an obligation towards her. Had even once expressed disappointment that she had not met him while she was still 'free'. Another word to set alarm bells ringing.

Because Silvia, though beautiful and entertaining, was hardly the material from which good wives were made. After all, she'd had no compunction about putting horns on the unfortunate Ernesto, and who was to say she would not do the same to another husband, given the opportunity?

Suddenly he could see the precipice yawning in front of him and knew that, for safety's sake, he needed to step back, and fast, while he still could.

For there was another reason why any kind of open scandal should be avoided, particularly at this moment. The quality of the Galantana brand of clothing had saved the company from the worst effects of the global recession—indeed, they were planning expansion—but for that they needed extra finance for more new machinery at the Milan factory, as well as buying another site for workshops near Verona.

Which was principally why he had accepted Silvia's dinner invitation, because he'd learned that Prince Cesare Damiano, head of the Credito Europa bank would be present, and not because he liked to live dangerously.

He and Prince Damiano had spoken briefly but constructively, and negotiations were now proceeding. And while the banker was a charming, cultivated man with a passion for rose growing, he was also known to be a stickler for old-fashioned morality.

Any overt lapse on Angelo's part could well blow the

deal out of the water, and delay would be costly in all kinds of ways.

So a period of celibacy was indicated. Irritating, he decided cynically, but a necessity. As, it now seemed, was his marriage, which would provide a safeguard as well as an expedient.

He drove into the security parking of his apartment block, and rode the lift up to the top floor. As he stepped through his front door, his manservant, Salvatore, was waiting to take his briefcase and discarded jacket.

'There have been two phone calls for Your Excellency,' he announced, lowering his eyes discreetly. 'Also a note has been delivered.' He paused. 'Will your *signoria* be dining out this evening?'

'No,' Angelo returned, looking moodily at the unmistakable pale mauve envelope on the hall table. 'I shall eat here. Something light, Salvatore. I am not very hungry.'

The other's eyes lit up. 'I have some good veal—which I will cook in a little Marsala, perhaps?'

'With a green salad,' Angelo agreed. He ran a weary hand round the nape of his neck. 'In the meantime, I think I'll take a sauna. Get rid of some of the kinks of the day.'

In his bedroom, he stripped then walked into the bathroom, grabbing a towel on the way, to the wooden cabin that opened off it. He poured a dipper of water scented with aromatic herbs on to the coals and, spreading his towel on the slatted wooden bench, stretched out, closed his eyes and let his mind drift.

If he was going to marry, he mused, there were a number of practical matters to take into consideration, the most urgent being living accommodation, because, convenient as it was to the Via Veneto and the Rome headquarters of Galantana, this apartment was also his bachelor pad, and due to its past associations, not a suitable place to bring his bride, although he had no intention of getting rid of it.

No, he thought, she would be far happier living on his estate in the hills just outside the capital, and it would be a better environment for the son he hoped for. Or it would be once the air of melancholy following the loss of his mother, which had dulled his own memories of a happy childhood and caused him to avoid the place in recent years, had been banished forever.

His father, turned by grief into a virtual recluse, had suddenly and quite unexpectedly begun a refurbishment programme on the villa itself three years before. It had gone into abeyance on his death, but the time had come, Angelo decided, for it to be revived and completed.

It was odd, he admitted to himself, to be making plans for a woman he didn't even know as yet, but, as the Contessa Manzini, she would soon learn the duties and responsibilities of her new status and, he hoped, the pleasures of it too as he had every intention of being both generous and considerate.

She might not have his love, the sweet and passionate emotion that had held his parents steadfastly in thrall to each other, because he doubted whether he was capable of such feelings, but he could and would offer her, at the very least, respect along with every material comfort she could wish for. And a decent show of ardour should not be too difficult to feign. Besides, if she was pretty enough, he might not have to pretend, he told himself, grimacing inwardly.

He'd stayed with friends in Tuscany the previous weekend, and partnered a girl called Lucia in an impromptu tennis match. Good legs, he thought judiciously, a figure that curved in all the right places, and dark eyes that had gleamed in his direction more than once. He had not asked for her telephone number but that was an omission that could easily be rectified with an email to his host.

On the other hand, each time she'd played a bad shot, she'd giggled and he'd begun to find this irritating. The thought of having to listen to it morning, noon and even night was not appealing.

He sat up abruptly, cursing under his breath. He was hardly perfect husband material, so why should he expect to find the perfect wife? And what made him think Lucia would even want him?

For once, and perhaps understandably, he was finding relaxation difficult, so he abandoned the sauna, showered briskly, pulled on jeans and a polo shirt and went to the *salotto*.

As he'd anticipated, both phone messages were from Silvia, requesting him to call her. And her letter proved to be in similar vein but rather more demanding, he noted, his lips tightening. Clearly his absence in Tuscany and his omission to contact her immediately on his return had not pleased her. She was becoming distinctly proprietorial, and although he would have his regrets at terminating their association, he realised he had no choice.

He did not belong to her, he thought coldly, pouring himself a whisky. To her, or any other woman, and he never would. He had seen what that could do. Had seen his father become a silent stranger, the heart and spirit torn out of him after his wife's death—little more than a sad ghost in a house which had once been filled with sunshine and laughter.

Had found himself, scarcely out of boyhood, excluded from his own grief in the face of his father's desolation.

And without the tenderness and support of Nonna Cosima, who had taken him into her own home, he would have been left very much alone.

As he emerged from the darkness of that time, he'd sworn that he would never allow anyone to make him suffer like that. And nothing had happened since to persuade him to change his mind.

His marriage would be a practical arrangement without illusions, he vowed silently, and he would set himself to make it work.

Therefore, as a beginning, he would decline Silvia's suggestion that as Ernesto would be away the following weekend, they should take advantage of his absence at some discreet *albergo* in the wilds of Umbria or Reggio Calabria.

Instead, he thought, crumpling the note in his hand, I will be spending the time in close consultation with the builders at Vostranto, so I shall call her tomorrow and make my excuses.

And after that, I shall also ask Ottavio for Lucia's phone number.

'No,' said Ellie. 'It's very kind of Madrina to invite me, but I've already made my plans for that weekend. I'm sorry, Silvia.'

'You don't sound it.' Her cousin leaned back in her chair, pouting. 'I suppose you're off to bury yourself at Nonna Vittoria's shack as usual.'

It might only be a small house, but it was hardly a shack, Ellie thought drily. And Silvia clearly hadn't thought so when she discovered that their grandmother's will had left Ellie in sole possession of what could be an eminently desirable property in a charming fishing village on a beautiful coastline. She had raged about the total unfairness of the bequest for weeks if not months, accusing Ellie of wheedling her way into Nonna Vittoria's good graces.

By which Ellie supposed she meant visiting her grandmother regularly and remembering her at birthdays and Christmases. Something Silvia's busy social life had overlooked most of the time.

'And how can you even think of it when you could be staying in the lap of luxury at the Villa Rosa?' Silvia went on.

'Perhaps I don't find the lap of luxury particularly comfortable,' Ellie said drily. 'Especially when I'm aware that I'm the only person present who's actually an employee instead of an employer.'

Silvia waved a languid hand. 'Oh, you're far too sensitive, *cara*. Besides Madrina adores you, and you owe her a visit. She has said so, and will be so upset if you refuse.' She paused. 'And you could do me the most enormous favour too.'

Ellie's hand stilled in its task of refilling their coffee cups. Ah, she thought, without surprise. Now we're coming to it.

She said, 'Oh God, Silvia, you haven't been losing money at bridge again, not after the things Ernesto said last time.'

'Oh, that.' Silvia looked down, playing with the emerald

and diamond ring on her wedding finger. 'I've hardly touched a card for months. Truly. Anyone will tell you.'

'Except that I don't know anyone to ask,' Ellie returned, scenting an evasion. 'And I have no money to bail you out, so don't even think about it.'

'That's not what I'm asking,' Silvia denied swiftly. 'It's just that—well—Ernesto is being a little silly at the moment about my going away without him, even to see my own godmother, and if he knew you'd be there too, I'm sure he'd change his mind.'

Ellie brought over the fresh coffee, placing the cup on the table beside her cousin's chair.

She said slowly, 'It's not like him to play the heavy husband. Silvia, you're sure that you're not the one who's being silly?'

Silvia flushed angrily. 'And what makes you an authority on married life? I wasn't aware that you even had a boyfriend.'

Ouch, thought Ellie, remembering at the same time that attack had always been Silvia's favourite form of defence. Also, that it had been several weeks since her cousin had sought her company—and then only at the last minute to make up the numbers at a dinner party, where, to add to her usual shyness, she'd felt badly dressed and totally out of her depth.

Especially when Silvia had been at her sparkling best, eyes gleaming like her jewellery, and her mouth curved on the edge of a smile all evening, and the centre of everyone's attention. As if, Ellie thought, a fire had been lit inside her.

In fact, on that occasion, Ellie had taken her godmother's place, as the Principessa Damiano had been suffering from a heavy cold. But at least she'd only had to give up a few hours—unlike this new request, where she'd be committed from Friday evening until late afternoon on Sunday. Not a prospect she relished, however fond she was of her tiny, exquisite godmother fluttering like a butterfly in the pale draperies she affected.

Although that, Ellie had always suspected, was just a façade, concealing a will of reinforced steel. Which was why she'd probably used Silvia to back up her invitation.

But Ellie was always conscious that Madrina inhabited a

world where Silvia belonged, but she herself did not. They might be first cousins, but chalk and cheese didn't even come near it.

Silvia, the elder by almost a year, was silvery fair, with green eyes that looked at the world from the shadow of extravagant lashes, a small straight nose and a frankly sexy full-lipped mouth. Her chief ambition from childhood had been to marry a rich man and she'd achieved it effortlessly, although Nonna Vittoria had frowned and tutted over her choice, murmuring that *cara* Silvia needed to be held in check, and that her *fidanzato*, though estimable, might not be the man to do it.

Ellie, on the other hand, had often thought, without rancour, that she resembled the negative of a dramatically coloured photograph. Her own hair was the shade generally known as dirty blonde, and she was pale-skinned and slender. Nonna Vittoria always told her she had unusual eyes, but the rest of her features were nothing to admire. Nose too long, she thought. Mouth too serious.

However, on the plus side, she enjoyed her work, liked most of her colleagues and had a small group of friends of both sexes with whom she ate out and attended films and concerts.

She supposed it was a relatively sedate existence, but it suited her. Yet so did her own company, and the times when she could escape to the coast and the waiting Casa Bianca were among her happiest.

She couldn't let the opportunity to spend the weekend there pass. Could she?

Yet, as she drank her coffee, she sent a covert glance at her cousin. Something was wrong. She knew it. The shining brightness of a few weeks ago had become restive—even edgy.

She said quietly, 'Silvia, I don't want us to fall out but I need you to be honest with me. Why do you want me to accept Madrina's invitation?'

Her cousin looked sulky. 'It is nothing. An absurdity. A man Ernesto feels has paid me too much attention. He has even started to think that I am meeting this man and not going to

Largossa at all. But if he knows that you and I will be at the Villa Rosa together, his mind will be at rest.'

Ellie frowned. 'Wouldn't it be simpler if he accompanied you himself?'

Silvia spread her hands. 'He cannot. There is a client—an important man—with tax difficulties which must be settled *pronto*. So Ernesto must handle the case personally, even if he has to use the weekend.'

Ellie could sympathise with the client's needs. Italy's labyrinthine tax laws were not for the inexperienced or the fainthearted.

And yet—and yet...

She recalled suddenly that she'd thought she heard the name of Alberoni mentioned in a low-pitched conversation by the water cooler at work a few weeks ago, only to find when she joined the group that they were talking about something completely different.

Now she found herself wondering uneasily if the subject had been deliberately changed at her approach and just what they'd been discussing.

If the stolid Ernesto had been stirred to a seething mass of jealousy, might he have reason? Whatever, he seemed to be taking steps to keep Silvia in check at last, and maybe, as her cousin was all the family she had left, she should help, besides having no wish to hurt her godmother's feelings by a refusal to attend her house party.

'Who else will be there?' she asked cautiously.

Silvia shrugged. 'Oh, Fulvio Ciprianto and his wife.' She added casually. 'Plus one of Madrina's elderly cronies, the Contessa Manzini.'

Manzini, thought Ellie. The name was vaguely familiar, but in what context? Then her mind went back to that wretched dinner party, and she remembered. A man, she thought, tall, very dark, and lethally attractive even to her untutored gaze, who'd been pointed out to her as Count Angelo Manzini. Not, she'd reflected at the time, that he looked even remotely like an angel. The lean saturnine face, amused dark eyes and mobile, sensuous mouth suggested far more sin than sanctity.

However, no playboy apparently, but the successful chairman of the Galantana fashion group, or so she'd been informed by her neighbour during a brief lull between courses.

Which, considering what she'd been wearing, was probably why the Count had totally ignored her.

'A few others, perhaps,' Silvia went on, twisting the emerald on her finger again. 'I am not sure. But if you get bored,' she added with renewed buoyancy, 'you can always ask Zio Cesare to show you his roses. You like such things.'

Ellie had never addressed her godmother's august husband as 'uncle' in her life, and Silvia knew it. Another reminder of the wide gap in their circumstances.

'Thank you,' she returned ironically.

'So I can tell Madrina that you will be coming with me, Ella-Bella?' Silvia was watching her almost eagerly.

But, thought Ellie, there was another element in her expression that was not so easy to fathom, and which sparked a faint *frisson* of concern.

'Only if you swear never to call me that stupid name again, Silly-Billy. We're no longer children,' she retorted crisply. 'And I'll telephone her myself.' She paused. 'Shall we go in my car?'

Silvia looked as horrified as if Ellie had suggested they trudge to Largossa, pushing their luggage in a wheelbarrow. 'You mean that little Fiat? No, I will arrange for Ernesto to lend us the Maserati with Beppo to drive us.'

Ellie frowned. 'He won't want them himself?'

'He has the Lamborghini.' Silvia pursed her lips. 'Or he could walk. The exercise would do him good, I think.'

'Poor Ernesto,' said Ellie.

And poor me, she thought when her cousin had departed, leaving a delicate aroma of Patou's 'Joy' in the air. Although that, she admitted, was rank ingratitude when she would be staying in a superbly comfortable house, with magnificent food and wine, and being thoroughly indulged with her godmother's unfailing affection.

But it was simply not the kind of visit she was accustomed to. Usually she was invited to keep Lucrezia Damiano company while her husband was away attending meetings with other European bankers. Sometimes, but not always, Silvia came too.

But Ellie could not imagine why her cousin was so keen for them both to attend what seemed to be a distinctly middle-aged party.

Oh for heaven's sake, she adjured herself impatiently, as she carried the coffee pot and used cups into her tiny kitchen. Stop worrying about nothing. It's not a major conspiracy. It's simply a couple of days out of your life, that's all.

And when they're over, you'll be straight back to the old routine again, just as if you'd never been away.

Then she paused, as she began to run water into the sink, staring into space as she wondered exactly what it was that Silvia wasn't telling her. And why she should suddenly feel so worried.

CHAPTER TWO

'*CARISSIMA!*' Lucrezia Damiano embraced Ellie fondly. 'Such a joy.'

Ellie, partaker of a largely silent drive from Rome in the back of the Maserati, with Silvia, face set, staring moodily through the window, had yet to be convinced of the joyousness of the occasion, but her godmother's welcome alleviated some of the chill inside her.

The Villa Rosa had begun its life at the time of the Renaissance, and, with additions over the centuries, including a small square tower at one end, now had the look of a house that had simply grown up organically from the rich earth that surrounded it. The Damianos possessed a much grander house in Rome, but Largossa was the country retreat they loved and regularly used at weekends.

The *salotto* where the Principessa received her guests was in the oldest part of the house, a low-ceilinged room, its walls hung with beautifully restored tapestries, furnished with group-ings of superbly comfortable sofas and chairs, with a fireplace big enough to roast a fair-sized ox.

The long windows opened on to a broad terrace, and offered a beguiling view of the grounds beyond, including the walled garden where Cesare Damiano cultivated the roses that were his pride and joy.

But her host, Ellie learned, would not be joining the party until the following day.

'My poor Cesare—a meeting in Geneva, and quite

unavoidable,' the Principessa lamented. 'So tonight will be quite informal—just a reunion of dear friends.'

She turned to her other god-daughter, who was standing, her expression like stone. *'Ciao, Silvia mia. Come stai?'*

'I am fine, thank you, Godmother.' Silvia submitted rather sullenly to being kissed on both cheeks, causing Ellie to eye her narrowly.

She didn't look fine, she thought. On the contrary, since she entered the house, Silvia appeared to be strung up on wires. Nor had it been lost on Ellie that, on their arrival, she had scanned almost fiercely the cars parked on the gravel sweep in front of the villa's main entrance as if she was looking for one particular vehicle before sinking back in her seat, chewing at her lip.

'And now there are people you must meet,' the Principessa decreed, leading the way out on to the terrace.

An elderly lady, dressed in black, her white hair drawn into an elegant chignon, was seated at a table under a parasol, in conversation with a younger, plumper woman with a merry face, but they turned expectantly at the Principessa's approach.

'Contessa,' she said. 'And my dear Anna. May I present my god-daughters—the Signora Silvia Alberoni, and Signorina Elena Blake. Girls, allow me to make the Contessa Cosima Manzini and Signora Ciprianto known to you.'

The Contessa extended a be-ringed hand to both, murmuring that it was her pleasure. Her smile was gracious, but the eyes that studied Ellie were oddly shrewd, almost, she thought in bewilderment, as if she was being assessed in some way. If so, it was unlikely that her simple button-through dress in olive-green linen, and the plain silver studs in her ears would pass muster. And nor, she imagined, would her very ordinary looks.

The Contessa, by contrast, was not only dressed in great style, but her classic bone structure still suggested the beauty she must have been in her youth.

They took the seats they were offered, and accepted glasses of fresh lemonade, clinking with ice. Silvia seemed to have come out of sulky mode and was talking brightly about the journey, the warmth of the day, and the beauty of the gardens, her smile expansive, her hands moving gracefully to emphasise some point, while Contessa Manzini listened and nodded politely but without comment.

Under the cover of this vivacity, Ellie found herself being addressed quietly and kindly by Anna Ciprianto, and asked, with what seemed to be genuine interest, about her work at the Avortino company, so that she was able to overcome her usual shyness with strangers and chat back.

After a while, Lucrezia Damiano went off to greet more guests, a couple called Barzado, also middle-aged, the wife bright-eyed and talkative, whom she brought out to join the party.

So what on earth am I doing here? Ellie asked herself in renewed perplexity. And, even more to the point, what is Silvia?

On the surface, her cousin was brimming with effusive charm, the very picture of the lovely young wife of a successful man, but Ellie could see that her posture was betrayingly rigid, and the hands in her lap were clenched rather than folded.

I want to help, she thought, wondering why, when she and Silvia were together, she so often felt like the older one. But how can I—if she won't talk to me—won't tell me the problem?

And at that moment she saw the Contessa look down the terrace, a hand lifting to shade her eyes, as the faint austerity of her expression relaxed into warmth and pleasure.

'Mio caro,' she exclaimed. 'Alla fine. At last.'

Ellie did not have to look round to see who was approaching, and whose tall shadow had fallen across the sunlit flagstones. Because one glance at Silvia, her eyes wide and intense, her natural colour fading to leave two spots of blusher visible on her cheekbones, suddenly told her everything she needed to know, making her realise at the same time that it was information she would far sooner have been without. And that all her concerns about this weekend were fully justified.

Nor did she need to wonder further about the whispers round

the coffee machine, either in her workplace, or probably any other.

'Oh God,' she whispered under her breath, dry-mouthed with shock. 'I don't believe this. Silvia—you complete and utter fool.'

'My dearest one.' Count Angelo Manzini, contriving to look elegant in chinos and an open-necked white shirt, bent to kiss his grandmother's hand, then her cheek. 'Ladies.' A brief, charming smile acknowledged everyone else at the table, but bestowed no special attention anywhere.

Ellie had the curious sensation that the air around them had begun to tingle, and hastily drank some more lemonade, keeping her eyes fixed firmly on the ground, as he pulled up a chair and joined the group.

In daylight and close up, he was even more formidable, she thought, taking a deep steadying breath, and wishing with all her heart that she was back in Rome. Or that Silvia was.

She wondered if she could invent some emergency to provide her with an excuse for leaving, only to remember, with a sinking heart, that she had inadvertently left her mobile phone on charge back at her apartment, and that any landline calls to the villa would be answered by Giovanni, the major domo, and relayed through the Principessa herself.

So it appeared she was stuck here for the duration.

Lucrezia was speaking. 'My dear Count, I know you are acquainted with Signora Alberoni, but I believe you have not been introduced to her cousin, my other god-daughter, the Signorina Elena Blake.'

'No, I have not had that pleasure. I am charmed, *signorina.*'

Ellie sat up with an alarmed jolt, forcing herself to look at him, and murmur something polite and meaningless in return. His mouth was unsmiling, but his dark gaze that met hers held a faint glint that might have been amusement. Or—equally—anger.

Though what he had to be angry about defeated her, she thought, glancing away, her own expression stony. After all, she was the one who'd been manipulated into providing cover for his affair with Silvia. But if he imagined she'd have come within miles of the Villa Rosa if she'd known the truth, then the glamorous Count Manzini could think again. And, she told herself almost grinding her teeth, if he actually thought it was funny…

As soon as she could do so, she excused herself on the grounds she needed to unpack and went indoors, feeling as if she'd escaped.

There was never any question about which room she'd be using. Since her first childhood visit, when she'd gazed entranced at the little tower, telling her amused godmother that it was like something out of a fairy tale, that had been where she'd slept.

But as she climbed the spiral staircase leading up to it from the little sitting room below, she reflected that, mercifully, the Principessa no longer teased her that she was waiting for some princely hero to leap up the other steep flight of exterior steps from the garden to the small balcony outside her window and carry her off.

On the contrary, in recent years, she'd come to regard the tower room in much the same light as the Casa Bianca—as something of a refuge, and probably it would never be more so than this time, she thought with a troubled sigh as she contemplated the afternoon's developments.

Unlike Silvia, Ellie had only brought one small case, so her unpacking was soon completed, but she had no intention of returning to the terrace, even though it would probably be expected of her.

Instead, she used the tiny adjoining bathroom to shower away the stickiness of the journey, and, she vainly hoped, some of its subsequent tensions. Then, wrapped in her white cotton robe, she curled up in the small deeply cushioned armchair in front of the open window and resignedly gave full rein to her uneasy thoughts.

She would be having severe words with Silvia, once the opportunity presented itself, she promised herself grimly. Her cousin had no right—no right at all—to implicate her even marginally in whatever was going on between herself and that diabolically good-looking bastard who'd just swanned in.

Not that there were any real doubts in her mind about the situation—how could there be?—which suggested that, if Silvia wasn't careful, other people including Madrina, would be drawing the same conclusions.

And Silvia must be mad if she thought her godmother, or, more particularly, the austere Prince Damiano would tolerate any possibility of open scandal under their roof.

And while she could admit that maybe Ernesto was not the most exciting man in the world, she remembered how Silvia had insisted she wanted to marry him and no-one else. Or was it more the status of being a rich man's wife she'd actually hankered for?

Whatever—there was a limit to Ernesto's placidity, and if he even suspected that Silvia had been unfaithful to him, there'd be trouble bordering on catastrophe.

How could her cousin take such a risk—especially when it did not seem to be making her happy? Ellie asked herself in bewilderment. But remembering her original assessment of Count Manzini, she doubted whether bestowing happiness would be a priority in his relationships anyway.

Here today, she thought, biting her lip, and gone tomorrow. Not that she was any real judge of such matters, of course, but instinct warned her he was the kind of man anyone with sense should cross a busy street to avoid.

But there were no busy streets at the Villa Rosa, as Ellie discovered several hours later when, to her horror, she found she'd been placed next to Count Manzini at dinner.

It was punishment, she thought, for fibbing to her godmother that she'd stayed in her room with a slight headache instead of rejoining the party.

Nor was it any consolation that the Count seemed no more pleased at having her as a neighbour than she was.

Because Madrina had emphasised an informal evening,

Ellie had kept back the long dress she'd brought in deference to the Prince's known wishes, choosing instead a pretty georgette skirt in white, patterned with sunflowers, which floated around her when she moved, and a scooped-neck silk top, also in white. Neither of them were from the Galantana line, as she was sure one quick glance had told him.

She had no idea who'd made his expensive suit either, but decided it was probably Armani.

At the other end of the table, Silvia was resplendent in a royal blue cocktail dress, made high to the throat in front, but plunging deeply at the back. She seemed to have recovered her equilibrium—in fact she looked almost glowingly triumphant—and was chatting with animation to her neighbours as if she didn't have a care in the world.

Leaving me free to do the worrying for her, Ellie thought, serving herself from the dishes of *antipasti* which began the meal.

She'd not yet had the chance for a private word with her cousin who'd been missing from her room at the other end of the villa when she went in search of her, leaving Ellie to wonder where she was and decide that she'd probably prefer not to know.

'May I offer you some tomato salad?' Count Manzini enquired with cool politeness, and she looked up from her plate with a start.

'No,' she said, stiltedly. 'No, thank you.'

'I seem to alarm you, *signorina*,' he went on, after a pause. 'Or do you simply prefer to eat in silence?'

'I think—neither.'

'I am relieved to hear it.'

He smiled at her for the first time, and she felt her throat tighten nervously as she reluctantly experienced the full impact of his attraction. The government, she thought shakily, should issue a warning, and felt something like a grudging sympathy for Silvia.

'I believe we have encountered each other before, but were

not formally presented to each other,' he continued. 'One evening at the home of Ernesto Alberoni, I think.'

'Perhaps.' Ellie stared rigidly down at her food. 'I—I don't remember.'

'*Che peccato,*' he said lightly. 'Also, I was not aware that our hostess had more than one god child. Do you visit her a great deal?'

'As often as I can, yes.' Her tone was faintly defensive.

'And this weekend—it is an engagement of long standing?'

She wanted to say 'Hasn't Silvia told you how she dragged me down here at the last minute as a cover story?' but decided against it. On the other hand, she didn't see why she should answer any more of his questions.

She shrugged. 'I can't really remember when it was arranged,' she returned, deliberately casual. 'Does it matter?'

'Not at all,' he said. 'I am just a little curious about your presence at a party where the other guests are so much older.'

'But I'm not the only one.' She was careful not to glance in Silvia's direction. 'The same could be said of you, Count Manzini.'

'I am here because I have business with Prince Damiano,' he said softly. 'And when it is concluded, I shall be gone.'

Let it be soon, thought Ellie, helping herself to more anchovies and wondering at the same time if her cousin was aware of his plans.

When he resumed the conversation, he turned to rather more neutral topics, asking if she played tennis—she didn't—and if she liked to swim, at which point she claimed mendaciously that she hadn't brought her bathing costume.

He was being perfectly civil, yet Ellie was thankful when his attention was claimed by Signora Barzado, seated on his other side, and she was therefore able to relax a little and enjoy the *gnocchi* in its rich sauce, and the exquisite veal dish that followed.

It occurred to her that even if she'd been unaware of his involvement with Silvia, she would still not have felt comfortable with him. There was arrogance beneath the charm, she thought, suggesting that he regarded women as just another facet of his success.

Besides, he was in orbit round some sun while she remained completely earthbound.

Not that it mattered, she told herself, as she ate her *panna cotta* with its accompanying wild strawberries. Tomorrow he would leave and, with luck, she would never have to set eyes on him again. All the same she wished that Prince Damiano had not been detained in Geneva.

It was a long meal with strega and grappa to accompany the coffee which ended it, but when it was over and they drifted back to the *salotto*, Ellie's need to talk to Silvia was thwarted again by her cousin immediately opting to play bridge with Signora Barzado and the Cipriantos.

Count Manzini, to her relief, took himself off to the billiard room with Carlo Barzado, while his grandmother and the Principessa occupying a sofa by the fireplace had their heads together in low-voiced and plainly confidential conversation.

Ellie found a magazine in a rack beneath one of the side tables, and took it to a chair on the other side of the room. It was mainly concerned with the fashion industry, and, inevitably, had a feature on Galantana praising its success and detailing its anticipated expansion. This was naturally accompanied by a photograph of Angelo Manzini seated at his desk, his shirt sleeves rolled back over tanned forearms and his tie loose. He looked tough, business-like, and, as even Ellie could appreciate, sexy as hell.

The camera, she thought, drawing a breath, was no doubt being operated by a woman.

At the bridge table, one rubber followed another and Ellie was forced to accept that Silvia was avoiding any kind of *tête à tête* between them, and she might as well go to bed.

'So soon, *cara*?' The Principessa regarded her with concern. 'It is not still the headache?'

'Oh, no,' Ellie assured her swiftly and guiltily. 'That seems to have gone.'

In her room, the bed had been turned down and her white lawn nightgown prettily fanned across the coverlet, but the helpful maid had also closed the windows for some abstruse reason, turning the room into a temporary oven.

Sighing a little, Ellie opened them again, drew the curtains, and switched on the ceiling fan. She took a quick cooling shower, cleaned her teeth, then folded back the coverlet to the bottom of the bed, deciding for once to dispense with her nightgown before sliding under the cover of the sheet.

She'd arranged to leave the Avortino office early that day, so she'd brought some remaining translation work with her to finish off. It was a simple enough task, and normally she'd have whizzed through it, but this time she found it well-nigh impossible to concentrate, and after struggling for almost an hour, she gave up.

If I go on, I'll have a genuine headache, she thought, putting the script back in its folder, then switching off her lamp and composing herself for sleep instead.

She lay for a while, staring into the darkness, listening to the soft swish of the fan above her, while the events of the day played through her mind like a depressing newsreel. And most disturbing of all was the number of unwanted images of Angelo Manzini that kept intruding upon her.

She tried to tell herself it was hardly surprising, considering that blinding moment of unwelcome revelation about Silvia and its possible repercussions. But it was troubling nevertheless.

On the other hand, there was no point in losing sleep over it, so she turned on to her side, closing her eyes with resolution.

He should not, Angelo told himself grimly as he glanced at his watch, be contemplating this.

Having made the break, he should adhere to his decision and not be lured back, even if it was for 'one last time' as she'd breathed to him in that secluded corner of the garden before dinner. When she'd stood so close that the shape of her untrammelled breasts under the cling of her dress were clearly revealed, the nipples standing proud. So close that the familiar perfume she wore filled his senses, reviving memories that commonsense told him were best forgotten.

Although he knew of her relationship with the Principessa, he'd been frankly astonished and certainly not best pleased to find her here. In view of the serious purpose of his visit, she was a complication he did not need.

And yet when she'd looked up at him wistfully, touching her parted lips with her little pointed tongue, reminding him of its delicious artistry, and whispered, 'Don't you want me, *mio caro*?', in spite of himself, he had found his body responding to her enticement with all its former urgency.

All the same, he would have drawn the line at traversing unfamiliar corridors to reach her, in the hope that the other members of the house party—his hostess in particular—would be safely asleep.

But as this would not be necessary, the promise of 'one last time' seemed worth the risk.

No-one, he told himself, would be likely to see him descending from the *loggia* outside his room, especially now he'd changed his white shirt for a thin dark sweater.

But if the worst happened, he could always explain he'd been unable to sleep, and decided to get some air.

Or, he could take the infinitely wiser course of resisting temptation altogether, and staying where he was. However disappointed his former *innamorata* might be, she could hardly make a scene over his dereliction. Not in this company.

And afterwards, he would be careful to avoid any encounters with her until she had found the inevitable someone to take his place.

Counsels of perfection, he thought cynically. Which he had, *naturalmente*, no intention of following. Not while that gloriously rapacious body was waiting to welcome him on this hot, starlit night.

Earlier, he'd fetched the flashlight from his car, and sliding it into his pocket, he went noiselessly out to the *loggia* and down the steps to the grounds below.

* * *

Ellie was never sure what woke her. For one sleepy moment, she wondered why, on such a still night, the pale curtains at her window seemed to be billowing into the room? Only to discover, with blank terror, that she was no longer alone. That a tall shadow, darker than all the rest, was standing beside the bed and a man's voice was whispering teasingly, 'Were you asleep, *mia bella*? Then I hope you were dreaming of me.'

Then before she could move or force her paralysed throat muscles to scream, the mattress beside her dipped under a new weight, and strong arms reached for her, drawing her against bare and aroused male flesh while a warm mouth took hers in the kind of deep and sensual kiss wholly outside her experience.

And for one brief, appalled instant, she felt her ungiven body arch against him in a response as instinctive as it was shocking.

Then, as sanity came racing back, she tore her lips from his and tried to push him away, raking her nails down the hair-roughened wall of his torso.

He swore and his grasp slackened fractionally, giving her the chance to fling herself across the bed away from him, her hand reaching desperately for the lamp switch.

And as light flooded the room, Ellie's horrified, incredulous gaze met that of her assailant.

Angelo was the first to speak. He said hoarsely, 'You? But I don't understand...'

'Get out of here.' She was blushing from head to foot, burning with shame, as she delved for the sheet, dragging it up to cover her naked breasts. Trying at the same time not to look at him. 'Just—go. Now. For God's sake.'

But it was too late. There was a sharp knock at the door, followed by her godmother's voice saying, 'Is all well with you, Elena? An intruder has been seen in the garden.'

Angelo muttered something soft and violent under his breath, and dived for the sheet in his turn. And before Ellie could answer, think of some reassurance to send her latest visitor away, the door was flung wide, and the Principessa came in, swathed in an ivory silk dressing gown. And behind her, dignified in grey satin, the Contessa Manzini, with Carlo Barzado beside her, and Giovanni bringing up the rear.

Lucrezia Damiano stopped, a hand flying to her throat, her eyes widening in shock and dismay. There was a long and deadly silence, which the Contessa was the first to break, turning to request Signor Barzado and the gaping major domo to leave before she too stepped into the room, closing the door behind her.

She said, '*Cosa succede*, Angelo. What is happening here? Have you lost your mind or simply all sense of honour?' She looked at Ellie, her face like stone. 'Is my grandson here at your invitation, *signorina*? The truth, if you please.'

Angelo answered for her. 'No,' he said. 'From first to last, Nonna, it was my own idea.' He glanced down at the scratches on his chest, his mouth twisting wryly. 'But clearly, I should have thought again—for several reasons.'

'You are saying you have disgraced our family name—forced yourself on this girl—on a whim?' The Contessa closed her eyes. '*Dio mio*, I cannot believe it.'

It occurred to Ellie that hoping to wake up and find she'd simply been having a nightmare wasn't working. Neither was praying for death.

Clutching the sheet so tightly that her knuckles turned white, she said huskily, 'Contessa—Godmother—I know how this must look but—really—nothing happened.'

'I presume because he was interrupted.' The Principessa's voice was colder than her god-daughter had ever heard it, as she looked pointedly at Ellie's nightgown lying on the floor beside the bed.

No, Ellie thought painfully. Because he discovered he was in the wrong room, with the wrong woman.

Thought it, but realised she couldn't say it because it would only make matters a thousand times worse.

Angelo indicated his own clothing. He said coolly, 'Perhaps, before anything more is said, I might be permitted to dress myself.'

'*Tra un momento.* My god-daughter's needs come first.' The Principessa took Ellie's robe from the chair and advanced to the bed. 'Put this on, my child, then come with us to the *salotto*.' She added, 'You will have the goodness to join us there, Count Manzini, when you are ready.'

Back turned to him, and seated on the edge of the bed, Ellie huddled awkwardly into the robe and fastened its sash, her fingers all thumbs. She was suddenly aware that she was trembling, and on the verge of tears.

It's all so ridiculous, she thought, like some dreadful bedroom farce. Except that on this occasion there can be no last act explanations to make everything right again. Because they would have to involve Silvia, and that can't happen.

As she followed the two older women downstairs, her mind went into a kind of overdrive as she struggled to make sense of what had happened.

It went without saying that Angelo Manzini had expected to find her cousin waiting for him, but Silvia's room was at the other end of the villa, so what could possibly have made him think she was sleeping in the tower?

And what was all this about an intruder in the grounds? Who had seen him?

Every question she asked herself seemed to throw up another, and she didn't like any of the answers that were suggesting themselves to her.

Giovanni was just leaving the *salotto* as they arrived. His face might be expressionless, but he radiated disapproval just the same and Ellie, who'd known him all her life, found herself avoiding his glance.

He'd lit the lamps and brought a tray of coffee to the room, and the Principessa poured a measure of brandy into a glass and brought it to Ellie.

'I have instructed Giovanni to have another room prepared for you,' she said. 'You will not wish to return to the tower.'

No, thought Ellie, with a swift pang. Never again for as long as I live.

Any stupid fairy tale dreams I still had finally crashed and burned tonight.

Aloud, she said, 'Thank you,' and swallowed some of the brandy, feeling its warmth pervade the chill inside her. 'But I swear to you—both of you—that nothing happened.'

'You regard my grandson's shameful conduct—this outrage to your godmother's hospitality as nothing?' The Contessa's question was icy. 'Are you saying, *signorina*, that you are accustomed to share your bed with strangers? That this unforgivable insult should be—laughed off in some way? Treated as one of the aberrations of modern life? If so, I doubt if Prince Damiano will agree with you.'

Ellie flushed again. 'No,' she said, her voice constricted. 'No, of course not.' She hesitated, 'Does he—have to be told?'

'I think so,' said the Contessa. 'Before the story reaches him from another source.' She paused. 'It is unfortunate that Carlo Barzado witnessed what had happened, because he will tell his wife, and she will immediately tell the whole world.'

Ellie's lips parted in a soundless gasp. 'Oh—surely not.'

The Contessa shrugged. 'It is inevitable.'

The Principessa sat down beside Ellie, and took her hand. She said more gently, 'We must suppose that Count Manzini gave some indication—at dinner, perhaps—that he found you attractive, my child, and you were flattered by his attention. Gave him reason to think that you would welcome him later. Is that how it was?'

Ellie bit her lip. The truth was impossible, she told herself, so she would have to rely on prevarication.

She said quietly, 'If I did, it was—unintentional.'

'But I think we must accept that was the case and act accordingly.' Her godmother's tone was firm. She looked towards the door. 'I am sure Count Manzini will agree.'

Coming into rooms silently must be one of his talents, Ellie thought bitterly because she'd been totally unaware of his arrival—yet again. But there he was, leaning against the doorframe, the lean body apparently relaxed, his dark face impassive as he listened to what was being said.

But Ellie wasn't fooled. The anger in him might be dammed back, but she could still sense it. Feel it reaching her across the room.

But why, she demanded silently, when I'm the innocent party in all this? And you know it.

Angelo walked slowly forward. 'I deeply regret, Signorina Blake, that I completely misunderstood the invitation I thought I had received.' His mouth twisted harshly. 'It was an unforgivable error, and *naturalmente*, I wish to make amends for my behaviour in any way that is suggested.'

'My dear Angelo,' said his grandmother. 'In view of Prince Damiano's known moral stance, you have only one course of action. Tomorrow, *mio caro*, to prevent further scandal, you will announce that you and Signorina Blake are engaged to be married.'

CHAPTER THREE

ELLIE'S HAND JERKED and the remains of her brandy splashed down the skirt of her robe.

She said in a voice she hardly recognised, 'No. I can't—I won't do it. It—it's crazy. I tell you—nothing happened.'

'I believe you.' Lucrezia Damiano took the glass from her hand. 'And if only you had been seen by no-one but the Contessa and myself, there would be no problem.' She sighed. 'But my dear Cesare, I fear, will adopt a very different attitude.

'Promised lovers carried away by their feelings, he might accept, although he would certainly not approve. But a casual encounter based on a passing attraction, and conducted in his house?' She shuddered. 'That he would find intolerable.' And paused, adding, 'Unforgivable.'

Ellie could feel the tension in the room crackling around her like an electrical storm.

'I'll talk to him,' she said wildly. 'Somehow make him understand...'

'But, dear girl,' said the Principessa. 'What could you possibly say?'

And in one thunderstruck moment, Ellie realised that both her godmother and the Contessa knew perfectly well exactly where and with whom Angelo had really planned to spend the night.

That they'd probably been aware of the situation for some time.

But that, even if it was not a secret, it would still not be spoken of openly, because discretion had to be observed at all costs.

Which, in the short term, she was being called upon to pay. And her silence was only the first instalment.

She bent her head. 'Nothing,' she said wearily. 'I suppose.'

'You show good sense,' the Contessa remarked. She looked calmly at her grandson. 'You have not spoken, Angelo *mio*.'

His tone was icy. 'Perhaps I am lost for words.'

'*Tuttavia*, I am sure you appreciate the necessity. Your negotiations with Prince Damiano will go more smoothly if you undertake them as Signorina Blake's *fidanzato*, rather than her attempted seducer. I am certain you must agree.'

'Under the circumstances, it seems I have little choice,' he said with an undisguised bitterness that made Ellie send him a surprised glance from beneath the veil of her lashes. He added with chilling clarity, 'And an engagement is not a marriage.'

Excuse me, Ellie wanted to say indignantly, but just who is doing the big favour here and to whom? Because, Count Angelo Manzini, I wouldn't want you if you came gift-wrapped.

And tried to put out of her mind the sudden searing memory of the way his mouth had moved on hers with such devastating sensual purpose, and her own shocked, aching reaction.

'Then the matter is settled,' the Principessa said briskly, and rose. 'Now I suggest we try to get some rest for what is left of the night.' She paused, then added pointedly, 'Let us hope there will be no further alarms to disturb us.'

Ellie did not find the remainder of the night particularly restful. Her belongings had already been transferred to her new room, thanks to the supremely efficient Giovanni, whom, she thought shuddering, she never wanted to look in the face again. She had to admit that the accommodation was more luxurious than the tower room and possessed a very much larger and very comfortable bed for its occupant to sink into.

But she could not relax. She had far too much to think about, little of it pleasant. For one thing, it was clear that she and Angelo Manzini had been deliberately set up, and almost certainly by Silvia, but what she couldn't figure was—why?

For another, as she'd turned at the door of the *salotto* to say 'Goodnight', she'd found him watching her go with an expression of such scornful resentment that she'd felt her skin burn under his regard.

Anyone would think, she'd thought angrily, as she went upstairs, that I was the one having the illicit *affaire*, instead of him. But whatever problems he's having, he's brought entirely on himself, and he has no-one else to blame.

Plus he must know the last thing I ever wanted was to become involved with him or any of his sordid little games, so a touch of gratitude wouldn't come amiss.

Nor could she escape the terrible irony that the first time she'd found herself in bed with a man was only as a result of mistaken identity. She supposed it was almost funny, yet she had never felt less like laughing in her life.

The entire situation had been total humiliation, she thought as pain twisted inside her, turning rapidly into complete disaster.

She lay in the darkness, her mind revolving wearily over the same well-trodden ground, trying to make sense of it all and failing miserably.

Wondering too how she would get through the horrific difficulties of the day ahead, pretending to be engaged to a man who appeared to despise her.

She could find no answer to that and there were already pale streaks in the eastern sky when she eventually fell into an uneasy sleep.

It was mid-morning when she was woken by one of the maids bringing her a breakfast tray of tea with lemon, warm rolls, ham and cheese. At least she was being spared the gauntlet of the dining room, she thought, as the memory of Signor Barzado's face, goggle-eyed with shock, invaded her shuddering mind. But that had to be the least of her worries.

She ate what she could, then showered quickly and dressed.

She paused to look at herself in the full-length mirror before venturing downstairs, scrutinising her ordinary dark green linen skirt and very ordinary white tee shirt. That said it all, she thought, grimacing at her reflection. And no-one in their right mind would ever believe that a man like Angelo Manzini would ask her to marry him, or steal through the darkness for a secret night of passion in her arms.

However, that was the story, and she would somehow have to stick to it. But only for a strictly limited period, she told herself, lifting her chin. Which was probably the sole aspect of the situation that she and Count Manzini were likely to agree on.

Giovanni was waiting as she descended the stairs, inclining his head respectfully as he told her the Principessa wished her to be shown to her private sitting room.

No real surprise there, Ellie thought drily. It was a charming retreat, furnished in shell pink, a shade her godmother described as 'most calming to the nerves', and where no-one else would dare to go unless specifically invited, so their conversation would be undisturbed.

When they reached the door, Giovanni tapped deferentially, then ushered her in. Ellie walked in, a smile nailed firmly in place, only to stop dead as the room's sole occupant turned from the window to face her.

He was wearing charcoal pants this morning, and a matching shirt open at the neck. Against the sunlit pastel background, he looked as dark as a moonless night, making Ellie feel, absurdly, that this pretty room was no longer a sanctuary but a panther's den.

It was all she could do not to take a step backwards, but she recovered herself and said quietly and glacially, 'I thought I was here to speak to my godmother, Count Manzini.'

'She felt we should have an opportunity to meet alone.' His tone was casual. 'And as we have to convince the world we have been doing so quite intimately over the past weeks, it might be better if you addressed me as Angelo. And I shall call you Elena.'

It was all said without smiling, but at least he wasn't looking at her as if she was a slug in his salad. Cool indifference seemed an appropriate description. And she would match it.

She lifted her chin. 'Then you really intend to go on with this—ridiculous pretence?'

'Unfortunately, yes.' He paused. 'It was mentioned last night, I think, that I am here to negotiate an important financial deal for Galantana with Prince Damiano. There is a great deal at stake, and I will not allow my plans for a major expansion of the company to be wrecked by the malice of an angry woman.'

She said quickly. 'Angry?'

'You were aware, I suppose, that your cousin had been my mistress?'

'No, I wasn't,' she snapped. 'Not until you arrived yesterday and I saw her reaction.'

'Ah,' he said. 'Then you also will not know that I ended the relationship two weeks ago.'

'Ended it?' She stared at him. 'That wasn't the impression you gave last night.'

'It was to be the last time,' he said, shrugging. 'And one doesn't wish to disappoint a lady.'

'Really?' Ellie's tone bit. 'Maybe you should have remembered the risk you were running a little earlier and stayed in your own room.'

'Hindsight,' he said, 'is a miraculous gift. Besides, the invitation I received was—most pressing.'

Her face warmed as she recalled just how sure he'd been of his welcome. 'I—I really don't want to hear about it.' She took a deep breath. 'And I still can't believe that Silvia's done this. I—I had no intention of spending the weekend here. I only came because I was concerned about her.' She spread her hands. 'Even if she wanted revenge by setting you up, why did she have to involve me? It's unbelievable.'

His voice was expressionless. 'She may have had a reason.'

'Well, I can't imagine what it could be.' Ellie paused. 'Anyway, how did she know you'd be here?'

He frowned. 'I probably mentioned it, when it seemed not to matter. I forget.'

'A costly lapse.'

'As you say.' His mouth hardened. 'But, believe me, I would have remembered if she had said she was also to be a guest—and changed my plans accordingly.'

Ellie said slowly, 'Once she'd talked me into it, of course, her scheme just—fell into place. I can see that now. After all, you'd have no means of knowing that the tower room was always given to me.'

'No.' He gave her a considering look. '*Infatti*, its isolation seemed to make it ideal for a place of assignation.' He paused. 'How did she persuade you to come with her?'

She bit her lip. 'She said Ernesto was becoming foolishly jealous and she needed me to be a kind of chaperone.'

'*Dio mio*.' His mouth tightened. 'And instead she made you her *ingenuo*—her fall guy.'

'Yes.' She hesitated. 'I presume she was also the one who gave the alarm about the supposed intruder.'

'But of course,' he said. 'And with impeccable timing.'

She swallowed. 'If you say so.' Her flush deepened. 'But surely you—you must have known that you weren't—that I wasn't…?'

'Not until you drew blood.' His smile was sudden and mocking. 'And maybe not even then, although it is usually my back that suffers.'

If she blushed any more, she would probably burst into flames, Ellie thought, setting her jaw. 'Then it's a pity you didn't realise your mistake at once,' she said icily. 'And spared us both some hideous embarrassment as well as this present ghastly mess.'

'How true,' he said. 'But a man with a warm, naked girl in his arms does not always think clearly, you understand.'

No, thought Ellie. She did not understand, but she did not intend to cause him further amusement by saying so.

She said stiffly, 'You seem to be taking this very lightly, Count Manzini.'

'Do I?' There was an edge to his voice. 'You would be entirely wrong to think so, Signorina Blake. I accept the situation we have been forced into because I must. But, believe me, I shall not forget the cause.'

He paused. 'Tell me something. Why, last night, didn't you tell the truth about my presence in your bed?'

She said in a low voice, 'Perhaps if Madrina had been alone, I'd have done so, and the whole thing could have been—hushed up. But there were other people there—your grandmother—Signor Barzado. I couldn't let them know that you thought I was really Silvia.'

His mouth curled cynically. 'Your loyalty is as touching as it is misplaced.'

She said stiltedly, 'What you don't realise is that she's been—good to me. Generous too with things like—clothes.'

'And the scent you wore last night,' he said softly. 'Was that also a gift from her?'

'Why, yes. It was almost a full bottle. She said she no longer cared for it.' She gave him an uncertain look. 'How did you know?'

'A fortunate guess,' he said. 'Pour the rest away, *signorina*. It does not suit you, as I am sure she knew.'

'But it wasn't just Silvia,' she added unhappily. 'There were her parents to consider as well. They've always been so kind to me.' She hesitated. 'And—Ernesto, too, in his way. He doesn't deserve to be hurt like this.'

He shrugged. '*Prima o poi.* Sooner or later, it will happen, but I, *grazie a Dio*, shall not be the cause.'

He moved away from the window, walking towards her, and this time she did step back, her eyes meeting his defensively. He halted, the dark brows lifting in hauteur.

He said, 'Perhaps I should remind you that we are supposed to be passionately in love. So much so that we forgot everything in our need to be together.'

'Who on earth is going to believe that?' she muttered defensively.

'No-one—if you intend to flinch each time I come near you,'

he returned tersely. 'Everyone—if you stand with your hand in mine and smile at me while our engagement is announced. And, most importantly, Prince Damiano will believe it.'

'But is that really so important? There must be other banks you could approach if Credito Europa turns you down,' she protested.

'In the financial world, a rejection by Cesare Damiano would be taken very seriously,' he said. 'It would be a black mark not just against me but Galantana too. I cannot permit that to happen.'

He added harshly, 'This trick that Silvia has played on us is like a stone dropped into a pool. The ripples are already beginning to spread. I discovered this at breakfast when I encountered Signora Barzado's prurient gaze. She cannot wait to leave, I think, and tell all Rome how we were caught *in flagrante.*'

Ellie looked down at the carpet. 'Your grandmother believes that too.'

'*Bene.* It follows that we must give the lady another less interesting story to spread.' He added sardonically, 'One with a happy ending.'

'It can hardly be called that.' She swallowed. 'More a tissue of lies.' She hesitated. 'And just how long will we have to maintain this deception?'

'For as long as it is necessary.' He shrugged. 'Believe me, *signorina*, you are not the only sufferer.'

He glanced past Ellie as the door opened to admit the Principessa, her smile a little fixed.

'You must excuse me. I have been welcoming another guest. Silvia's husband, *caro* Ernesto, has been able to join us. Such a pleasure.' Ignoring Ellie's gasp of disbelief, she paused, playing with the bracelet she was wearing, her glance flickering from one impassive face to the other, now flushed with anger as well as embarrassment.

'And by now you have arranged everything between you, I am sure,' she went on. 'The Prince has telephoned to say he will be here for lunch, so I suggest the announcement is made then.'

But nothing happened...

The same desperate words echoed and re-echoed in Ellie's head, but remained unuttered. There was no point, she thought numbly. A course of action had been agreed, and would be adhered to. Ernesto's sudden arrival had guaranteed that. But what had brought him? Had he come of his own accord, or had it already been arranged with Silvia? And had the important client who needed his advice ever existed?

She felt too weary to think any more, as she watched Angelo Manzini bow slightly, kiss her godmother's hand then leave.

The Principessa came over to her, studying her with critical eyes. 'You look a little worn, dearest girl. If you go to your room, my maid will bring you this wonderful concealer that I have discovered and show you how to use it. You must look radiant for your *fidanzamento.*'

Ellie gave her an anguished look. 'Godmamma—I...'

Lucrezia Damiano kissed her on the cheek. 'And do not worry, my little one.' She gave a determined nod. 'All will be well. All will be very well. You will see.'

Consolata was deft and clever with cosmetics, Ellie was forced to admit. The face that looked back at her from the mirror was no longer as pale and strained as it had been. Her lashes had been darkened with mascara, and her mouth defined by a soft coral lipstick.

The older woman had frowned and sighed, however, over the limited choice of clothing in the wardrobe and reluctantly agreed that the skirt and top Ellie was already wearing would have to do.

But the *signorina* was not to go immediately to the *sala da pranzo*, she added. The *Principe* had returned and wished first to speak to her in the garden.

Ellie's heart sank, but she supposed the interview with Cesare Damiano was inevitable.

She found him as usual in the walled garden among his

beloved roses, a tall man with iron-grey hair, treading slowly along the graveled walks, his gold-rimmed glasses on his nose as he scanned the beds for signs of disease or pests.

As Ellie reached him, he turned from his scrutiny of a magnificent display of blooms so deeply crimson they seemed almost black.

'The *Toscana*,' he said meditatively. 'As beautiful as when it was first grown here six hundred years ago. It gives one a sense of stability—of the rightness of things. Do you not think so, Elena?'

'Yes, Your Highness.'

He studied her gravely. 'Your godmother tells me that you and Count Manzini wish to be married, my child.'

That, thought Ellie, startled, is the last thing either of us wants.

Aloud, she said hesitantly, 'We—we have agreed to become engaged, sir.'

He pursed his lips. 'An engagement is a solemn promise and, in this case, made not before time, according to what my wife has told me.' He sighed. 'And while I deplore the way your courtship has been conducted, I believe I must give you both my blessing.

'I have spoken to Count Manzini,' he went on more briskly. 'And he has assured me there will be no more unseemly incidents before the ceremony. Nevertheless, young blood runs hot, and the Principessa and I agree that you should at once take up residence in our house in Rome, and be married from there. That should remove temptation and at the same time dispel any unfortunate rumours.' He allowed himself a faint smile. 'I shall allow myself the privilege of giving you away, my dear child.'

The world seemed to recede to some far distance. She was aware of the sun beating down on her head, and the hum of bees. And from somewhere, her voice saying hoarsely, pleadingly, 'But there's no need for so much hurry—surely.'

The austere look returned. 'I hope not indeed. But at the

same time there is also no reason to delay.' He glanced past her. 'As I am sure your *fidanzato* will wish to assure you.'

Ellie turned apprehensively to see Angelo Manzini approaching unhurriedly down the path.

Prince Damiano patted her shoulder. 'I will leave you together. But first—this.' He reached out and picked a long-stemmed red rose from a nearby bush. 'A flower for lovers,' he said, handing it to her, then, bowing slightly, walked off towards the house.

She watched him go, almost in despair, then turned to face Angelo, her slim body rigid, her eyes blazing accusation.

'You seem disturbed, *mia bella*,' he commented coolly as he reached her.

'I'll say I'm disturbed,' she said shakily. 'This engagement is quite bad enough, but they seem to be planning our wedding as well. What the hell is going on?' She drew a breath then added furiously, 'And I'm neither yours, nor am I—beautiful.'

'Not when you are glaring at me, perhaps. And your choice of clothing hardly does you justice either.' He paused. 'But you have possibilities, as I observed last night when you were wearing no clothes at all.'

For a moment she was lost for words, then she said chokingly, 'How—how dare you?'

He shrugged. 'You chose to turn on the lamp. And I am not blind.'

'No,' she said fiercely. 'And you also have the power of speech, so go back to the house right now and tell them it's all off. That I've turned you down.'

'That would be foolish,' he returned unmoved. 'Particularly as we have the Prince's approval—in addition to our other well-wishers.'

'What do you mean?' Ellie demanded huskily.

His smile did not reach his eyes. 'Come, *signorina*. You cannot be that naïve. Or that stupid. You must know that Silvia is not the only conspirator at Largossa this weekend.'

She said, 'And I tell you that I haven't a clue what you're talking about. Now will you do as I ask?'

'No,' he said. 'Because it would solve nothing. *Infatti*, it would simply make matters infinitely worse. I have already explained to you why I need the Prince's goodwill. Can you afford to have it withdrawn? You are fond of your *madrina*, I think. Do you really wish to be barred from her house and denied her affection? Because that would follow.

'More than that,' he added grimly. 'How will you like being known as my discarded lover? Is that the kind of notoriety you desire? And do you truly want your cousin to enjoy her unpleasant victory and laugh at us both? Because I do not.'

'But—marriage.' She pronounced the word with something like revulsion.

'*Grazie,*' Angelo returned coldly. 'However, I have no more wish than you to put my head in that noose. For the moment, there will be an engagement only.' He paused. 'But engagements can be easily broken. It happens every day. We have only to choose some convenient moment.' His mouth curled. 'And I will make certain that the fault is mine. Some flagrant act of infidelity, perhaps, to make the world think you have had a fortunate escape.'

Ellie took a breath. 'Count Manzini, you have the morals of an alley cat.'

'While you, *signorina*, have the tongue of a shrew. Shall we agree that we are neither of us perfect? *Nel frattempo*, in the meantime, I offer you this.' He produced a small velvet-covered box from his pocket and opened it.

Ellie looked down at the square antique sapphire set amidst a blaze of diamonds and swallowed.

'I—I can't wear that.'

'You are allergic to precious stones?' He sounded mildly interested.

It would have been childishly rude to retort, 'No, only to you,' so she refrained.

'I simply couldn't accept anything as valuable,' Ellie said, and frowned. 'How come you're carrying something that expensive around anyway?'

'It belongs to my grandmother,' he said. 'She promised that

when I planned to marry, she would allow me to choose a ring from her collection for my *fidanzata*. I picked this one.'

'But you did not pick me,' Ellie said. 'And you have no plans to marry—anyone. As the Contessa knows perfectly well. So this is sheer hypocrisy.'

'No,' he said. 'It is part of our agreement. Now give me your hand.' He met her defiant eyes, and added, *'Per favore.'*

She stood in silent reluctance as he slid the ring over her knuckle. She wore little jewellery at the best of times and none at all on her hands, and it felt heavy—even alien.

She was still holding the rose that the Prince had given her, and its fragrance, exquisitely sweet and sensuous, drifted upwards in potent contrast to the bleakness of the moment.

'Do you have any further instructions for me?' she asked bitterly.

'Instructions, no,' he said. 'But perhaps—a suggestion.' And took her in his arms. For a moment, sheer astonishment held her still as his lips plundered hers in a hard, draining kiss without tenderness or, she recognised with shock, any real desire.

Then, as she began to resist, he let her go. He said softly, 'Your mouth is the colour of that rose, *mia bella*. At last you look as if you know a lover's touch. So, now let us do what we must.'

CHAPTER FOUR

AFTERWARDS, IT WAS the faces she remembered. The Contessa, impassive; her godmother beaming but with anxious eyes; Signor Barzado trying to hide his astonishment and his wife her disappointment that a potential scandal had been overtaken and diluted by convention; the Cipriantos, astonished too but pleased.

And above all Silvia, seated beside her clearly bemused husband, her lips stretched in a smile, but her eyes burning with anger as Prince Damiano made the announcement with grave pleasure, and Angelo took Ellie's hand, glowing with the blue fire of his sapphire, and raised it formally to his lips.

The lunch had been sumptuous, but she'd eaten like an automaton, hardly tasting a mouthful. Then there'd been the toasts to be got through, her mouth aching in an effort to smile and acknowledge the good wishes, whatever their level of sincerity.

Standing rigidly to receive Silvia's air kiss on both cheeks, then watching her turn to Angelo with the husky murmur, 'Congratulations, *mio caro*. How truly clever you are.'

Being lost for words as Ernesto, after wishing her joy without the slightest conviction in his voice, had said, 'This is very sudden, Elena. I wasn't aware you were even acquainted with Count Manzini.'

And discovering Angelo at her side, smiling as he replied, 'But I have you to thank, Signor Alberoni. I saw her first at a dinner party at your house. Now—here we are.'

Later, feeling her face warm in a blush of sheer embarrassment as she again listened to Angelo courteously parrying the jovial demands to know when the happy day would be. Asking herself why she should be surprised, when talking himself out of dodgy situations was probably an everyday occurrence for him?

Now, at last, finding solitude in her room, with the shutters closed against the profound afternoon heat. And the door locked. An unnecessary but instinctive precaution. Because she was still trembling inside from the unexpected brush of Angelo's lips on hers as he escorted her to the stairs and his whispered, 'Soon we will be sharing the siesta, *mia carissima*.' And knowing his remark had been pitched at the world at large and that he didn't mean a word of it hadn't affected her reaction in the slightest. Which, in retrospect, worried her a little. Or rather more than a little.

Telling herself not to be stupid, Ellie turned restlessly on to her side and tried to relax. Her rose had been rescued from the lunch table by Giovanni and was now in a slim glass vase beside her bed. Something else she could have done without, she thought, as its evocative perfume reached out to her again, bringing with it unwanted and frankly dangerous memories.

Warning her that the coming days and weeks—she prayed it would be no longer—might well be some of the most difficult of her life.

Her most immediate problem, she realised sombrely, was the suggestion, fast turning into a decree, that she take up residence in the Damiano *palazzo* in Rome in order to prepare for her wedding. And, of course, to avoid any further sexual temptation before the legalised union of the wedding night.

It was almost funny, but she'd never felt less like laughing.

She could only hope that the Principessa would come to her rescue and use all her considerable powers of persuasion to convince her husband that such precautions were quite unnecessary, without stating precisely why this was so.

I just want my own life back, she told herself with a kind of desperation. My apartment, my work, my friends, and, more than anything, Casa Bianca, my house by the sea. If I'd only stuck to my guns and spent the weekend there, I'd have been spared this nightmare.

But even this won't last forever, and then I can start to be happy again.

And tried to ignore the small insistent voice in her head warning her that her life had changed forever, and, however hard she tried, nothing would ever be the same.

The dress she'd brought to wear for dinner that evening was new, ankle length in a dark blue silky fabric, with cap sleeves and a crossover bodice, the slenderness of her waist accentuated with a narrow band of blue and gold silk flowers. As she put it on, she realised, to her annoyance, that its colour matched the Count's sapphire almost exactly. As if it had been planned in advance, she thought with an inward groan.

She wished with all her heart that she could change it for something crimson—or magenta, or even bright orange—but she didn't possess as much as a scarf in any of those colours. Nor could she bring herself to wear the sunflower skirt two nights running.

The concealer that Consolata had left for her did its work again, and her freshly washed hair shone as it curved gently round her face, so, in spite of her inner confusion and anxiety, she looked relatively composed when she went down to the *salotto*.

Giovanni was waiting in the hallway to open the door for her, and she paused, drawing a deep breath, feeling as if she was about to walk onstage without knowing what play she was in, let alone any of the lines she was supposed to say. But the major domo's discreet smile and nod of approval helped launch her into the room, even if the sudden hush that met her appearance was disconcerting enough to induce a wave of shyness to sweep over her.

For a moment, she wondered if she was late, but one swift glance told her that she was not the last arrival. That neither Ernesto nor her cousin were yet present. No doubt Silvia was waiting as usual to make a last minute entrance in something by Versace that would knock everyone sideways.

I just wish I could do the same to her, she thought grimly.

'My dear.' Prince Damiano walked towards her. 'How charming you look.' He turned to Angelo who had accompanied him. 'You are a lucky man, Count.'

'I am well aware of exactly how fortunate I am,' Angelo returned silkily. His lips were smiling, but there was no accompanying warmth in the dark eyes as he took Ellie's unresisting hand and kissed it lightly. '*Mia bella*, Nonna Cosima is anxious to be better acquainted with her future grand-daughter. May I take you to her?'

His choice of words made her heart miss a beat. 'Yes,' she said huskily, recovering herself. 'Yes, of course.'

The Contessa was seated on a sofa, chatting to Signora Ciprianto, who rose to make a tactful retreat at Ellie's approach.

'I have brought you my treasure, Nonna,' Angelo said lightly. 'I am sure you will be as delighted with her as if you had chosen her yourself.' He paused as the Contessa bit her lip and changed colour slightly, then turned, smiling, to Ellie. 'May I get you something to drink, *mia cara*?'

There was something going on here, Ellie decided. Something she didn't know about, and probably wouldn't like.

Sudden anger shook her, and with it a desire to be perverse. She met Angelo's gaze limpidly. 'Oh, just the usual, please.' And being rewarded with a swift flash of annoyance in his eyes, she added, 'Darling,' as he turned to walk away.

The Contessa leaned forward and took her hand. 'Elena—I may call you that, I hope, and you must say Nonna Cosima. We have met in difficult circumstances, but we must now put them behind us and look instead to the future, and to happiness. Do you agree?'

Ellie was taken aback. The Contessa was speaking as if there'd been a slight glitch, now sorted out to everyone's satisfaction, when she knew—she must know—that the contrary was the case.

She said quietly, but with emphasis, 'The whole thing can't be forgotten too quickly as far as I'm concerned. And please believe that is something I absolutely look forward to.' She added stiltedly, 'I hope that's the reassurance you want.'

There was a glint in the dark eyes that struck Ellie as far too reminiscent of the lady's grandson. 'Not precisely,' said the Contessa. 'But it will serve for now.'

And then she began, with great charm, to ask questions. If Ellie had ever thought it was only the Spanish who had an inquisition, five minutes with Angelo's grandmother would have convinced her that the Italians weren't far behind.

She found herself speaking with total candour about her parents, her friends, her work at the publishing company, revealing, she realised, probably more than she wished. And, finally, she told the Contessa about her apartment.

When she mentioned she lived there alone, the Contessa's delicate brows rose. 'Then the sooner you accept the invitation to move to the Palazzo Damiano the better, dear child.'

Ellie sat up very straight. 'I see no need for that. Besides I love my apartment. It's my home.'

'But not for much longer. After all, you are going to be married, and you will share your husband's home.'

Ellie's hands clenched together in her lap. 'And—when I get married, I will do so.' *Or if...* 'But until then, I'll stay where I am.'

'Yet surely you must see that is impossible.' The Contessa sounded almost coaxing. 'Angelo could not be permitted to visit you there.' She gave a resolute nod. 'From now on, there must not be as much as another whisper of scandal about your relationship with my grandson.'

And as Ellie's lips parted to tell her without mincing her words that visits from Count Manzini did not feature on her personal agenda, and that there was no relationship with him—neither past, present nor future—she heard Angelo's voice saying coolly, 'Your drink, Elena *mia*. Campari with a splash of soda.' Adding softly, 'Just as you like it, *carissima*.'

Of course, Ellie thought, almost grinding her teeth. He'd have asked Madrina. As I should have known.

Accepting the glass from him, with a murmured, *'Grazie,'* she wished very much she could throw the drink at him, drenching the open mockery in the dark face and staining, perhaps irrevocably, his immaculate dress shirt as well. Before, that is, she left the room, screaming.

As it was, she took immediate refuge behind a wall of reserve, returning only monosyllabic replies to any remarks made to her, and thankful to her heart when the Prince, his wife and the rest of the party came to join them, and conversation became general.

It was when Giovanni announced respectfully that dinner was served that she realised that the group was not complete.

She said in an undertone to the Principessa, 'But, Madrina, Silvia and Ernesto haven't come down yet.'

'They are not here, *mia cara*.' Her godmother conveyed the news almost casually. 'Silvia felt that she was developing a migraine—so painful, so debilitating—therefore Ernesto took her back to Rome. Such a good and caring husband.

'But do not concern yourself about your own return,' she added brightly. 'Cesare has already said that you will travel with us. At the same time, arrangements can be made to bring your things from your *appartamento*. Which makes everything so very convenient, don't you agree?'

No, Ellie didn't agree, but she knew, through experience, that there was no point in saying so. Not once Prince Damiano had spoken. And since when had Silvia suffered from anything like a migraine?

It's like trying to find your way out of a maze, she thought bitterly as she made her way to the dining room. Every way you turn, you come up against a blank wall.

But later, when she looked up and found Angelo watching her across the silver and crystal of the polished dining table, his dark gaze frankly speculative, it occurred to her that blank walls might be the very least of her troubles.

As an object lesson in discovering how the other half live, Ellie soon realised, residence at the Palazzo Damiano could hardly be bettered.

She walked on marble floors from one massive, high-ceilinged room to another. She slept on the finest linen sheets, and her delicious food was served on delicate porcelain.

Her little flat would have fitted easily into the bedroom she'd been given alone, quite apart from the small but comfortable sitting room which led to it, and the luxurious bathroom which adjoined it.

And her second-hand Fiat screamed 'poor relation' when parked beside the Prince's limousine and her godmother's elegant Alfa Romeo on the gravelled sweep in front of the *palazzo*...

But when all this nonsense is over, she told herself staunchly, unlike so much else, it will be still around and still reliable.

And so, she hoped, would her job, even though her engagement had proved to be a nine day wonder at the office, to her acute embarrassment, while the sidelong looks from certain people had confirmed beyond doubt that rumours of Silvia's affair with Angelo Manzini had indeed reached the public domain.

In addition, one of the directors had called her in and asked outright at what point prior to her marriage did she plan to resign. Totally taken aback, she had flushed and stammered that she loved her work, and had no intention of abandoning it, and been answered by sceptically raised eyebrows, and the comment that her *fidanzato* might have very different ideas.

If I have to go on biting my lip each time he's mentioned, she thought savagely, I shall soon have no mouth left.

Even more galling was having to endure his actual physical presence at the *palazzo*, where he'd become a regular visitor, dining with them several times a week. And telling herself that his visits were only part of the pretence and that it was Prince

Damiano whom he really came to see made the situation no easier to bear.

He sent her flowers, too. Her sitting room was full of them.

And he kissed her. Mainly on the hand and the cheek admittedly, but sometimes on the lips—invariably when it was impossible for her to take evasive action.

Ellie supposed that nine out of ten women would have asked why on earth she would wish to avoid being kissed by one of the most attractive men in Italy, and found it difficult to explain, even to herself.

After all, she couldn't say that it was because she knew his kisses were prompted by duty rather than desire, when the last thing she wanted was for Angelo Manzini to desire her. Those brief moments in bed in his arms when she'd suddenly turned into a complete stranger had taught her that. And the memory of them still had the power to dry her mouth and make her tremble in a way that was totally outside her experience.

Which was where, she thought resolutely, she wished it to remain.

I must be one of nature's spinsters, she told herself, and derived no great comfort from this prosaic reflection.

She had not bargained either for being introduced to his relations. His Aunt Dorotea had been one of their earliest callers, a formidable matron who had given Ellie a searching look from head to toe then given an abrupt nod as if expressing satisfaction. Though what all that was about defeated Ellie entirely.

On a more positive note, Signora Luccino had brought her daughter Tullia with her, a girl with a sweet, merry face, married to a lawyer the previous year, and Ellie thought with regret that, under different circumstances, they might have been friends.

The Contessa Cosima, too, was a frequent visitor, alarming Ellie with a gentle flow of chat about churches and wedding dresses. That, she thought, was carrying pretence too far, and wished she had the nerve to say so.

In fact clothing had become an issue altogether. Her

wardrobe might be basic, she thought defensively, but it was perfectly adequate—a view that her godmother clearly did not share. The large *guardaroba* in her room was beginning to fill up with skirts, pants and tops in linen and silk, and a growing selection of evening wear in clear jewel colours and floating fabrics. And each outfit seemed to have its own shoes and bag in softest leather.

As if, she thought, scowling, it was not the done thing for Count Manzini to see her wearing the same thing twice.

She had tried to protest more than once that she was not a clothes horse, but the Principessa had waved these contentions away, smiling. It was her pleasure to see her dear Elena looking so lovely—and so happy too, she added brightly as Ellie's jaw dropped.

But there was no visit from Silvia. At first Ellie had thought that her cousin was quite understandably steering clear of her, only to be told by the Principessa that Ernesto, presumably in his role as good and caring husband, had taken Silvia for a little vacation on Corfu where his family had a house.

The days at the *palazzo* became weeks, and as they approached a month Ellie wondered how much longer the negotiations between Galantana and Credito Europa could possibly drag on, and when the deal would finally be done.

Because until that happened, she couldn't calculate how soon she'd be able to escape from this gilded cage, no matter how luxurious and loving it might be, and begin to reclaim her own life again.

More than anything, as the city heat increased, she missed the Casa Bianca and the breezes that blew from the sea, but her suggestion that she should spend some of her weekends there had been kindly but firmly declined. While her supposed engagement endured, it seemed she was going nowhere.

Surely it can't last much longer, she told herself each night with increasing desperation as she lay in bed staring up at the painted ceiling where gods and goddesses cavorted with unfeeling cheerfulness at some woodland banquet.

Worst of all, she'd noticed that one of the gods—probably

Mars—was black haired and dark eyed, his lean muscular body hardly concealed by the lion-skin thrown across one shoulder, and bearing a disturbing resemblance to Angelo Manzini. Or was that simply her over-active imagination?

Whatever, it wasn't an image she wished to find invading her bedroom all over again, but found to her acute annoyance that it still lingered in her mind, even when she turned over and buried her face in the pillow. Rendering her still more tongue-tied when she encountered the Count in the flesh, as it were, although he was always elegantly covered in some designer suit or other.

Another potent suggestion that the quicker she got out of there and back to sanity, the better it would be for her.

And each night she breathed the silent prayer. 'Oh please—please—let it be soon.'

Angelo stepped out into the heat of the Roman morning, as the automatic glass doors of the Credito Europa Bank whispered shut behind him. His face was calm as he walked to his car, taking his seat in the back with a murmured acknowledgement to the driver holding the door open for him, but this outward appearance was deceptive.

Because, underneath, he was blazingly, wickedly angry.

'Does Your Excellency wish to return to the office?' Mario asked with faint bewilderment as the silence lengthened.

Angelo pulled his thoughts away from the meeting he'd just attended, and met the chauffeur's enquiring gaze in the driving mirror. He said curtly, 'No, take me to my apartment.'

If Mario found this a strange request in the middle of a working day, it was not his place to argue. He dropped his employer at the main entrance, was told he would not be required again, then watched with a puzzled frown as Angelo strode inside.

The apartment was cool and silent, Salvatore as usual doing his marketing at that time of day. Which was good because Angelo wanted to be alone.

He walked into the *salotto*, impatiently stripping off his

jacket and tie, and tossing them over a chair. He unbuttoned his waistcoat, tore open the neck of his shirt, then poured himself a large Scotch, swallowed it, and poured another, even larger. He'd come home with the intention of getting blind, roaring drunk and wasting no time about it.

The news—no, the ultimatum—that he'd just received at the bank called for nothing less.

He could still hardly believe it. He thought he'd dealt with the trap that had been set for him at Largossa. Believed that simply going through the motions of courting the girl who'd been used in the snare—this Elena, Silvia's cousin and so much unlike his former mistress that she might have come from a different planet—would be enough to get him what he wanted, and he could then walk away. And that she would be equally grateful to see the back of him.

Dio mio, he thought. He'd almost felt sorry for her, recognising the reluctance of her co-operation. But no longer.

He walked to the sofa, flinging himself back against the cushions, taking another mouthful of Scotch, eyes narrowed, mouth compressed as he stared into space.

Now, too late, he recalled someone telling him when he was younger that Cesare Damiano had been nicknamed the Crocodile in banking circles.

Today the Prince had more than lived up to his name.

'My wife cares deeply for her god-daughter, Count, and is naturally concerned for the immense harm to her reputation if there were—consequences resulting from your liaison with her.'

He had sat on the other side of his polished desk, hands together, fingertips forming a kind of steeple, his expression grave as he studied the younger man. 'I am sure you understand me.'

And I, thought Angelo bitterly, fool that I am, I never saw it coming. Never understood that another trap had been set and was waiting for me. And while, if I'd used an atom of commonsense, I might have avoided the first, there is nothing I can do about the second.

Holy Madonna, I couldn't tell him there'd be no consequences as I'd simply been tricked into the wrong bed, or I'd
have found myself lying on the pavement outside, thrown there
by his security staff. And the consequences of that would be
truly horrendous.

Therefore if I want his money, I have to bite on the bullet by
accepting the eternally damned terms he spelled out to me with
such care, and somehow persuade the little Signorina Milk and
Water to become my wife. With the assurance that, once the
knot is tied, the finance will become immediately available.

He punched the arm of the sofa with his clenched fist.

Dear God, what a prospect, he thought despairingly. To
have to marry a girl who looks at me as if she'd come across a
snake sleeping in the sunshine. Who shrinks from my lightest
touch and answers me in monosyllables from surely the coldest
mouth in Rome.

But I know quite well it's not the Prince pulling the strings.
That I have his charming wife, plus my own grandmother, and,
of course, Zia Dorotea to thank for this current horror. All they
needed was the opportunity I was stupid enough to give them,
and my fate was sealed.

I must have been insane to think that an engagement would
be enough to satisfy them, he told himself. And perhaps I
should have asked myself too if their chosen candidate for the
post of my wife was really only the scapegoat she appeared to
be.

And, for a brooding moment, found himself remembering
a slim body warm against his and soft lips that had briefly
trembled beneath his kiss. Very briefly, he thought, because
the next moment, she had scratched him like a tigress.

Restively, he finished the whisky in his glass and set it aside.
Well if there was no other way to secure the promised loan,
and they all wished to transform Elena Blake into the Contessa
Manzini, he would oblige them.

But, he decided with icy resolution, she would have the title
and the status—nothing more, because she was the last woman

in the world he would have chosen for himself, and he had no intention of making her his wife in any real sense.

In fact, he told himself harshly, he would continue to seek his pleasures where he found them, though with rather more discretion in future, and he hoped they would all—the girl Elena included—be satisfied with the result of their machinations.

And as he had the phone number of an enchanting creature he'd met at a reception the previous week, instead of drinking himself into oblivion, he would call her right now and see if she was free for lunch, and whatever else the afternoon might suggest.

Starting, he thought with sudden grimness, as he meant to go on.

At first she couldn't quite believe what she was hearing. Didn't want to believe it, yet found herself listening numbly to what Madrina was saying so gently but with such total finality.

At last, she said, her voice shaking, 'I didn't even want to be engaged. You know that. But—marriage—to him! I couldn't—not possibly. And he—he doesn't wish it either. I know it.'

The Principessa patted her hand. 'But after what happened between you, the Count has to make reparation. Surely, you understand this.'

She sounded like the voice of sweet reason, Ellie thought, aghast.

'Your engagement must now be followed by a wedding,' her godmother went on. 'Quite apart from other considerations, our families bear two ancient names, and his own sense of honour as well as ours demands it. Besides it is high time he was married.'

She added with a note of reproof, 'You cannot have forgotten, dearest child, the exact circumstances under which you were discovered.'

'No,' Ellie said bitterly. 'Or the reason for it.'

The Principessa pursed her lips warningly. 'Put whatever you imagine out of your mind, Elena. It is of no use to dwell on something that cannot be altered.' She paused, then went on more briskly. 'Do not forget that Angelo Manzini is one of Rome's most eligible bachelors, and many young women would be glad to take your place at his side.'

Ellie wanted to say 'And they'd be welcome to him,' but something in the set of Madrina's mouth warned her against it.

Although that did not mean she was going to meekly submit to this new and frankly terrifying plan for her future. Far from it.

All this family honour stuff is like something left over from the Renaissance, she thought, seething. But I'm not a Damiano, and I have no intention of becoming a Manzini. My name is Blake and I make my own decisions.

So, I wouldn't have his glamorous Nobility as a husband, even if he came gold-plated and loaded down with sapphires.

He's well and truly off the hook, and so, thank God, am I.

CHAPTER FIVE

ON HIS ARRIVAL at the *palazzo* the following day, Angelo was informed by the butler that the Signorina was in the courtyard, and that it would be his honour to conduct the Count to her side.

So the purpose of his visit was clearly no secret, he thought grimly, as he followed in **Massimo's** stately wake, aware that his elegant silk tie seemed to be on the point of strangling him, and realising that, probably for the first time in his adult life, he was nervous about a meeting with a girl.

Although, of course, it was not just any meeting, as he swiftly reminded himself. So much—too much—depended on his ability to persuade her to his way of thinking, his personal reluctance notwithstanding.

The courtyard, at the rear of the *palazzo* was only small but pleasantly shaded by a lemon tree. The ideal setting, he supposed cynically, for such an encounter.

Elena, he saw, was sitting on the broad stone rim of the goldfish pond, her head bent, trailing her fingers through the water.

When Massimo announced him, she got to her feet in one hasty, almost clumsy movement, and Angelo realised that his own tensions at the coming interview were shared, if not exceeded.

At the same time, he saw that she was even paler than usual, her eyes shadowed and her lips pressed together as if to stop them trembling. She was more than tense, he thought with a jolt of shock. She was actually scared, and suddenly the wave of simmering resentment that had carried him here ebbed a little under the need to reassure her.

To explain, as well as he could, that the union being proposed between them would not include any of the usual physical obligations of being his wife. In fact, few constraints at all, if he could only make her believe him. And that she would spend their time together in all the comfort she could wish.

He walked slowly towards her, halting at what he hoped was a safe distance, unwilling to intimidate her further.

He said quietly, '*Buona sera*, Elena. *Come sta?*' He paused, and when she made no reply, continued, 'I think you have been told why I am here.'

'Yes.' Her voice was husky, her hands curling into fists in the folds of her very ordinary navy skirt. The plain white shirt she wore with it demonstrated she had not thought it necessary to adorn herself for the occasion, he thought sardonically.

She went on quickly, 'And I need you to know that I—can't. That what you ask is—quite impossible.'

'But you do not yet know what I want.' He kept his voice gentle. 'And that is what I wish to discuss with you now— alone and privately. An arrangement between the two of us that no-one else will hear of. Are you willing at least to listen to me?'

'There's no point.' She shook her head. 'I—I have to stop it now while I still can. They may have made you ask me, but they can't force me to say "yes" in return. Not in this day and age. It would be—barbaric. Even Prince Damiano would have to accept that.'

He said drily, 'I think, *mia bella*, that you overestimate the Prince's degree of tolerance. He expects us to be married. *Ecco*, a wedding ceremony will take place.'

'No,' Ellie said. 'It can't. I—I won't.'

'There is another man in your life perhaps?'

'No,' she said raggedly. 'But that's not the point.'

Sighing, Angelo walked over to her and sat down on the pond's stone surround, indicating with a brief gesture that she should join him. She obeyed mutinously, maintaining a more than decorous distance between them, making him suppress a flicker of irritation.

He said, 'Neither your wishes nor mine are the only consideration here, Elena. That is the real point, as I believed I had made clear to you.

'I have already committed myself to serious expenditure on my company's behalf on the basis of the financial package agreed in principle with Credito Europa. But unless you now become my wife, the package will be withdrawn and my dealings with the bank, which are already public knowledge, will be cancelled altogether with potentially disastrous results.

'Please understand that I have no intention of allowing such a thing to happen. Galantana provides a living for too many people in these difficult times, and I will not jeopardise my company's current success or the future of my workforce and suppliers while I have the power to avoid such a catastrophe.'

He looked at her, his mouth twisting wryly. 'You clearly do not want me as a husband. *Bene*. Let me be equally frank and say that I do not desire you as a wife.

'I suggest therefore that we regard our marriage as nothing more than a business deal—a temporary inconvenience that can be speedily concluded once Galantana's expansion has been paid for.

'As we shall be sharing no more than a roof, a discreet annulment can be arranged, and you will receive a generous settlement in return for your co-operation.' He smiled at her coaxingly, willing her to soften. 'So—what do you say?'

Stormy colour warmed her face. 'That it's the most flagrantly immoral idea I've ever heard, and you must be mad to think I'd ever agree.'

Angelo stayed silent for a moment, irritation warring with disappointment within him. She might be quiet, he thought, but she was certainly not biddable. He would have to be more direct in his approach.

'I think madness will be waiting for us if you refuse.' He allowed a grim note to enter his voice. 'If the deal with Credito

Europa fails, I shall have no reason to hide the truth about that night at Largossa. I shall tell Prince Damiano about the trick your cousin Silvia played on us both, and why, and point out that there is no reason for our engagement to each other to continue. I believe you can imagine what might follow.'

He bent and picked up a pebble from the ground, then dropped it into the water.

Ellie stared down as the ripples began to spread slowly but surely, becoming wider all the time.

It did not need any great exercise of the imagination, she thought bitterly. The consequences of Silvia's reckless behaviour had always been there, like shadows on the edge of a room. A very public divorce from Ernesto would probably be the least of it. The shadows would touch them all.

She said, 'This is like—blackmail.'

'Call it rather a matter of expediency.' His voice was level. 'If there is no marriage between us, the Barzados would no longer be silent, but rush to add their own embellishments to the existing gossip. Do you truly wish to be the centre of stories of midnight orgies at the Largossa estate, Elena? Be responsible for the damage to the Damiano reputation?'

'No.' She almost choked on the word. '*Certo che no.* Of course not.'

He shrugged. 'Then it can all be quite simply avoided. There will be a wedding ceremony and, after it, life will go on much as it does now, except that you will live at my house at Vostranto.'

He ignored her faint gasp and continued, 'It is quite large enough to accommodate us both without awkwardness. In any case, I intend to remain at my apartment in Rome during the week, so you will have little more of my company than you endure at present.' He smiled coldly. 'Perhaps less. And your nights you may spend alone with my goodwill. Let that be clearly understood.' He shrugged again. 'Then after an interval—a year, two years perhaps—we can set about dissolving the marriage, and you will be rich and free.'

As she hesitated, he added quietly, '*Elena, I beg you to*

think how much we both and others have to lose if you persist in rejecting me.' He paused. 'Believe me, if there was another choice to be made, I would take it.'

For a long moment, dizzy with uncertainty, she stared down at the flagstones at her feet, imagining them cracking apart, herself falling through the gap helplessly into some abyss.

In a voice she barely recognised, she said, 'You promise— you give me your word that you'll leave me alone. That you won't...' She broke off in embarrassment, not knowing what to say.

'I guarantee you will have nothing to fear from me.' His mouth twisted. 'I think our previous encounter was enough for us both.'

'Yes.' Her voice was small, stifled, as she tried hard not to think about those brief shocked and shocking moments, and the greater nightmare that had so swiftly followed. That still enveloped her in spite of his assurances.

And yet...

I do not desire you as a wife.

Words that were, perhaps not quite as comforting as they should have been. That—if she was totally honest—stung a little in their indication that she had somehow fallen short of a standard that was none of her making. That she had not even known was required of her.

'So may I tell the Prince that you have consented to be my bride?'

She lifted her head and looked at him, her eyes enormous in her pale face. 'If there is no other way, then I suppose—yes.'

His brows lifted mockingly. 'You are graciousness itself.'

'If you wanted a more generous reply,' she said, 'you should have asked a more willing lady.'

'On the contrary, Elena,' he said softly. 'I think you will suit my purpose very well.'

He reached for her hand and made to raise it to his lips, but Ellie snatched it back, flushing.

'Perhaps you'd restrict your overtures to those times when we have an audience to convince, Count.'

There was a pause, then he said courteously, 'Just as you wish, *signorina*.'

But Ellie knew that in that moment's silence she'd detected anger, like a flare of distant lightning, and even though she wrote it off as a typical male reaction to a dent in his machismo, she found the discovery oddly disturbing just the same.

They were married two weeks later at a very quiet ceremony held in the *palazzo*'s private chapel.

Ellie refused outright, despite all persuasions, to wear a conventional white gown and veil, and chose instead a silken slip of a dress, high-necked and long-sleeved in a pretty shade of smoky blue.

Signora Luccino looked at it askance, but her brows lifted in open disapproval when she heard that the pressure of work currently being experienced by the bridegroom had caused the postponement of the tradition *luna di miele*. Indefinitely.

'You astonish me, my dear Angelo,' she said majestically. 'I would have thought your new bride should take precedence over any matter of business.'

Angelo gave her a cool smile. 'You concern yourself without necessity, Zia Dorotea. Vostranto will provide us with all the peace and seclusion we could ever wish. Is it not so, *carissima*?' he added, turning to the new bride in question, who was silently praying for the entire farce to be over and done with, and as soon as possible.

The one bright spot in a hideous day, she reflected, had been the absence of Silvia, who was, it seemed, accompanying Ernesto to a conference in Basle.

But even that was small comfort as she stood before the ornate gilded altar listening to herself say the words that, in the eyes of the world, gave her to Angelo Manzini.

Now she could only blush vividly and murmur something incoherent that might have been assent to his question. Her awkwardness, however, did her no disservice either with Signora Luccino or any of the other guests. Indeed, her obvious shyness at the prospect of being alone with her glamorous husband was seen as charming.

Yet in an odd way Vostranto had become the least of Ellie's concerns about her unwanted marriage. The first time Angelo had taken her there, she'd sat beside him in the car, staring at the back of the driver's head, taut and unhappy as if she was on her way to jail.

The house itself was a surprise, an impressive pile of pale golden stone against the folded greenery of the foothills. It was roofed in green terracotta tiles and two massive wings reached out from the central building like arms outstretched in welcome, enclosing a gravelled courtyard where a fountain played in front of the lavishly carved doors of the main entrance.

Ellie stepped out of the car, and stood for a moment, relishing the warmth of the sun after the air-conditioning of the limousine, and watching the sparkle of the drops as a marble Neptune, his head thrown back in smiling triumph, endlessly poured water from an urn shaped like a shell.

To her own astonishment, she found her inner tensions begin to dissipate a little, even if the idea of the house welcoming her was clearly a figment of her imagination, and allowed herself to be escorted inside with more composure than she'd anticipated.

The entrance hall seemed vast and directly ahead of her a wide staircase made from the same marble as the floor led up to a broad half-landing carpeted in crimson, where it divided with two shorter flights of stairs leading up to twin galleries on either side.

'Your rooms will be in the West Wing,' Angelo informed her almost casually, nodding in that direction. 'Mine, in the East.' His smile was brief and did not convey much amusement. 'I hope that will provide enough distance between us to put your mind at rest.'

It occurred to Ellie suddenly—almost bleakly—that even if he'd said he'd be sleeping in the adjoining room to hers, there would still be a space like the Sahara Desert between them.

And had to catch at herself with faint bewilderment—because that was a good thing. Wasn't it?

Aloud, she said woodenly, 'You are very considerate.'

'I cannot take the credit.' He shrugged. 'The arrangement is a tradition.'

A pretty chilly tradition too, like all that insistence on family honour, Ellie decided silently as she followed him to the *salotto*. And could surely be dispensed with in this day and age. Although not on her account, naturally, she added hastily.

But one day, when they were free of each other, he would no doubt marry again, this time to a girl who would persuade him to rethink the sleeping arrangements because she wanted him close to her all night and every night.

And once more felt something she did not totally understand stir in the pit of her stomach.

The *salotto* was long and low-ceilinged, with a fireplace even bigger than the one at Largossa, suggesting how cosy the room could become in the depths of winter. But for now, the French windows at the far end stood temptingly ajar, inviting the occupants to step out on to the sunlit terrace beyond, and drink in the green lawns and flower beds she could only glimpse.

She'd been told the workmen engaged on the refurbishment had only left the previous day and she was aware of the scent of paint and fresh plaster in the air, and how the walls seemed to glow. She listened in silence to Angelo's cool and impersonal account of how the wiring had been replaced through the house, and all the plumbing modernised.

As if, she thought, he was delivering a lecture on the renovation of old houses to a not very interesting audience, instead of describing her future, if temporary, home.

From the *salotto*, they went to the dining room, with its superb frescoed ceiling, but by-passed altogether the room he referred to as 'my study' on their way to the kitchen quarters.

Which meant, she thought, that there were no-go areas for her too.

It was something of a relief to be delivered over to Assunta, his plump and smiling housekeeper, for the remainder of the tour, which, of course, included the rooms intended for her in the West Wing.

The bed, she supposed, swallowing, was also traditional, a huge canopied expanse of snowy linen, piled high with pillows, and a wonderful crimson coverlet with the Manzini coat of arms embroidered in gold.

But Ellie was aware of a swift jolt at Assunta's confidential disclosure that His Excellency had been born in that bed, accompanied by a twinkling glance to remind her where her own duty lay.

In the adjoining *stanza di bagnio*, as well as a deep, sunken bath, there was a semi-circular shower cabinet that would easily have accommodated the entire bathroom in her flat on its own.

And she would never, in a hundred years, have sufficient clothes to fill that panelled dressing room with its wall of wardrobes.

The entire set-up made her feel overwhelmed and even a little off-balance with the weight of its obvious expectations, especially when she'd realised from the first moment that almost everyone who worked in the house or on the estate was lurking in the vicinity in an attempt to catch a glimpse of her, and that the smiles that greeted her held unalloyed goodwill.

But then it was a long time, as Assunta had told her, the brown eyes suddenly a little anxious, since Vostranto had a mistress.

They're all going to be so disappointed in me, Ellie thought, as she returned downstairs to the unsmiling young man who was about to reluctantly bestow all this grandeur upon her.

She thought he'd be waiting for her in the *salotto*, glancing impatiently at his watch, but the room was deserted and she stood for a moment quite alone, relishing the quiet, reminding herself that this was how life was going to be for the foreseeable future, but also that she was used to it—accustomed, most of the time, to her own company both at her apartment and the

Casa Bianca—so that shouldn't, wouldn't be a problem. That really it was what she preferred.

And even as that thought took shape in her mind, everything seemed to change, as if, for a moment, this room into which she'd walked as a stranger only an hour or two before had become suddenly familiar and somehow—enfolded her.

So that when Angelo strode in from the terrace a few minutes later, looking preoccupied and asking if she was ready to leave, she agreed quietly and calmly, knowing that, when the time came, she would be even more contented to return. And that at least part of her life as the Contessa Manzini, while far from perfect, would at least be endurable.

But not all the issues within the marriage were going to be as easy to deal with. There was, for instance, the vexed question of her employment.

'My wife,' Angelo told her icily when she'd asked how soon after the wedding she could return to Avortino, 'does not work.'

Ellie gasped indignantly. 'But that's ludicrous,' she protested. 'Just what am I supposed to do all day—sit around twiddling my thumbs? Thank you, *signore*, but no thanks. I love my job, I'm good at it, and I've promised my boss that I'll be back at my desk—*pronto*.'

'Then you should have consulted me first, when I would have told you it was out of the question.' His expression was like stone. 'The matter is closed.'

'Like hell it is.' Her voice shook. 'I've agreed, much against my will and better judgement, to this pretence of a marriage. A little compromise on your part might be good.'

His lips tightened. 'If you think I am being unreasonable, Elena, consider the practical difficulties. Travelling into the city each day is only one of them.'

She lifted her chin. 'I have a car.' And I also had an apartment I could have used, she added silently, which you've made me get rid of, while keeping your own.

'I have seen your car,' Angelo said dismissively. 'Old and unreliable. A potential death trap, which will have to be replaced.'

He paused. 'But that changes nothing. You will have no time to spend at Avortino once you become the Contessa Manzini. Your predecessors have found that in itself a full-time job with a household to run. New duties to learn.'

'Well I can't speak for a long line of downtrodden women,' Ellie returned with equal coldness. 'But the household in question seems to have been managing perfectly well without either of us for some considerable time.'

'But that will change once we are married,' he said flatly. 'I intend to use Vostranto far more, and you will have to accustom yourself to being the hostess when I entertain friends—business acquaintances. That, I think, will take time.'

In other words, Ellie thought, slashed by a pain as sharp as it was unexpected, I'm not up to the job. As if I needed any reminder.

She said quietly, 'Then perhaps you should postpone your social whirl, Count Manzini, until I've gone back to the real world and you've acquired someone more suitable to welcome your guests.' She paused. 'I'm sure you'll be spoiled for choice.'

There was a silence, then he said slowly, 'Allow me to apologise. I did not intend how that must have sounded.'

Ellie looked past him, biting her lip. She said remotely, 'It really doesn't matter.' And wished with all her heart that her statement were true.

But, she told herself in silent defiance, if he thought the question of Avortino had been settled, he was entirely wrong. When this so-called marriage was concluded, she would need to work, having no plans to accept the proposed settlement however generous.

When it's over, I want it to be over, she thought. Which does not include being under any kind of obligation to him, legal, financial or otherwise.

However, she had not anticipated that Casa Bianca would prove yet another bone of contention.

The Principessa had mentioned it casually over dinner one

night. 'Your little seaside retreat, Elena. What will happen to that when you are married?'

Ellie hesitated, uncomfortably aware that Angelo, who had been talking to the Prince, had turned his head and was looking at her, brows raised in enquiry.

He said softly, 'A retreat for a new wife. That sounds a little alarming, *mia cara*. Also unnecessary. What is this place, and where?'

Ellie met his gaze, concealing her unease at the challenge in his voice. 'My grandmother left me a little cottage at the coast in a place called Porto Vecchio.' She added coolly, 'It's only a small fishing village, and not a bit fashionable, so I don't suppose you've heard of it.'

'No, but I have learned of it now, and the fact that you own a house there, which I was also unaware of.' He paused. 'It must involve you in considerable expense. I therefore presume you will wish to sell it?'

'On the contrary,' said Ellie. 'I have no intention of parting with it, although I may possibly rent it out in the holiday season.' *When hell freezes over.*

Angelo inclined his head courteously. 'All that is something we will naturally have to discuss.'

Ellie widened her eyes into a limpid stare. Allowed her voice a note of amusement. 'But, *mio caro*, what is there to talk about, when my decision has already been made?'

Besides, she added silently, Roman dictators went out with Julius Caesar, or hadn't you heard?

But the set of Angelo's jaw as he turned his attention back to the plate of *osso buco* in front of him, coupled with a long, thoughtful look from Contessa Cosima, warned her that she had probably not heard the last on the subject.

However, there was no way she was giving up the cottage, she vowed inwardly, no matter what objections her reluctant husband might have to her possession of it. It was her own special place and it meant too much—held too many memories to be abandoned on his say-so.

Nonna Vittoria had left a sum of money to cover immediate

maintenance costs and local taxes, but this, of course, would not last forever. And as Ellie had no intention of asking Count Manzini for a cent towards Casa Bianca's upkeep, retaining her job and its salary was becoming even more essential, she thought grimly.

But lying sleepless that night, an idea came to her that could solve that particular problem, although its accomplishment would probably not sweeten Angelo's temper.

On the other hand, there went a man far too used to getting his own way—especially with women. Maybe it was time he got his comeuppance, even in a minor way.

There was a room at Vostranto, not large but with good light, and not currently being used for very much, although there was a small kneehole desk under the window which, Ellie had been told, was where Count Angelo's late mother had written her correspondence and overseen the household accounts.

But if her laptop was installed there, she'd be able to receive translation work from Avortino by email, and return it, completed, by the same method. So commuting would not be necessary, and if she continued to use her maiden name for professional purposes, no-one need ever know that the new Contessa Manzini was gainfully employed, with or without her husband's goodwill.

She would need Assunta's help, but her instinctive response to Vostranto and the spell it had worked on her seemed to have established her firmly in the housekeeper's good books, so she did not foresee major problems from that direction at least.

Or, she reflected, turning over and punching her pillow into shape, just as long as there weren't too many references to the nursery accommodation on the second floor, also unoccupied.

But a week later, with the toasts drunk, the wedding cake distributed and the alien gold of Angelo's ring gleaming on her hand, Ellie was no longer so confident about winning the necessary concessions. After all, she reminded herself, she had basically been hired to do a job, so her status at Vostranto would be little more than that of an employee. And as she drove with her husband to her new home, this time without the chauffeur's presence, she could feel her inner tensions building again.

Glancing sideways, she saw that the tanned face with its sculpted mouth looked strangely austere, and realised he too must have reservations about the immediate future, and the sterile bargain it contained.

But it was all his own doing, she reminded herself stonily. I was just caught up in the subsequent storm. So whatever regrets he's having, he fully deserves.

And Silvia, of course, had got off scot-free as she'd done so many times in childhood when retribution threatened, proving that there was no justice. But Ernesto seemed to be keeping a close eye on her, so perhaps her wings had been clipped.

'Is something wrong?' Angelo asked suddenly, and she jumped.

'No. Why do you ask?'

'You seem a little restless.'

'Recent events,' she said, 'are hardly conducive to calm.'

There was a silence, then he said, 'I do not know what else I can say to assure you...'

'That I am of no interest to you?' Ellie lifted her chin. 'Believe me, *signore*, that is probably the least of my concerns.'

'Then what troubles you?'

She took a breath. 'There's something I have to tell you. I've decided to go on working—but from home—your home—from Vostranto.'

'How do you propose to do so?' His tone was not encouraging.

'By email. I—I've had a room your mother once used fixed up as an office.' She paused. 'It won't disturb you or get in the way of the household duties that seem so important to you. I'll work all the hours I need to for that. However, you must see that I need my career and my future.'

'You do not trust me to support you adequately?' He rapped the question at her.

'Yes—for the time being.' She swallowed. 'But try to understand that I also value my independence. Which will last a great deal longer than this—pretend marriage.'

He said something under his breath. Then: 'And you did not think to consult me before putting these arrangements—in place?'

'I thought of it—yes.' She stared rigidly ahead through the windscreen. 'But I decided I knew what you would say. And if you now countermand my instructions, then your staff will know that—as well as everything else—my wishes do not matter to you, which will make it difficult for me to gain their respect, and run Vostranto as efficiently as you seem to wish.'

There was another silence, then he said softly, 'I see I have underestimated you, Elena. On this occasion, I shall allow your orders to stand. But make sure—make very sure—that you do not underestimate me. I am still the master of Vostranto.'

'Of the house—yes.' Her heart was thudding wildly. 'But you're not my master, Count Manzini, and you never will be.'

He jerked the wheel suddenly, and Ellie cried out as the car veered to the side of the road, coming to rest on the grass verge.

'You like to challenge me, it seems, *mia bella*.' His voice bit. 'But you have done so once too often.'

He reached for her almost negligently, pulling her hard into his arms. His mouth was hard too, and sensually explicit, inflicting a kiss without mercy which left the softness of her lips bruised and burning when at last he raised his head.

His gaze was mocking, cynical, as he looked down at her.

'So, now you know, Elena, what it means to make me angry. You would be well advised not to risk it again. *Capisce*?'

She said in a voice she did not recognise, 'I—I understand.' And did not speak again for the remainder of the journey.

CHAPTER SIX

ELLIE STOOD, her arms wrapped almost protectively across her body, in the middle of the room she would now have to learn to call hers. Which made it, she thought, swallowing, no less imposing. Or daunting.

Besides being the only place in the house where she still felt like a stranger—an interloper.

That great canopied monolith was so obviously a marriage bed that she found herself wondering how many Manzini wives had lain there in the past waiting to perform their marital duties—something which, at least, she would be spared.

At the same time, her fingers strayed momentarily to her mouth, still tender and slightly swollen from the ravishment of his kiss.

She recognised, of course, that it had been foolish to provoke him, but his high-handed manner was enough to try the patience of a saint.

But, to her relief, he had not so much as glanced in her direction again until their arrival at the house, when he'd escorted her between the two rows of happily applauding staff to the door, lifted her into his arms and carried her across the threshold to more cheers and laughter.

And she'd forced herself to smile as if she was a real bride, and that this traditional ritual, ensuring she did not inadvertently trip or stumble on entering her new home, would actually bring her marriage good luck.

Good fortune, however, was the last thing on her mind. The

previous few days had been a strain, and now that it had all stopped, she felt tired and almost on the verge of tears.

She had been served coffee and delicious lemon-flavoured biscuits in the *salotto*, after which Angelo had excused himself with cool politeness and gone off to his study to read his emails.

Ellie, in her turn, was whisked upstairs by Assunta. She found, to her astonishment, that her cases had already been unpacked and their contents put away in the dressing room by someone called Donata, who was, it seemed, her personal maid, and who would return later to help her bathe and change for the evening ahead.

'But I don't want a maid,' Ellie protested. 'I wouldn't know what to do with one.'

'She will know,' Assunta said firmly. 'Besides for the wife of Count Manzini, it is most necessary. You will see.' She paused. 'And now, Contessa, you should rest before dinner.' However, her discreet twinkle as she departed suggested that it was the hours following dinner for which her young mistress should principally be refreshed and ready.

I'm such a fraud, Ellie thought wearily as the door closed behind the good woman. But, all the same, she had to admit the idea of a rest was appealing, although not on that enormous bed with all its implications which she would deal with when she had to.

However, there was a couch shaped like a particularly luxurious *chaise longue* by the shuttered window which would answer her requirements perfectly.

Ellie removed her shoes, her tights and, carefully, her dress, revealing the exquisite lingerie—bra, briefs and half-slip—also in soft blue silk, that she wore beneath it, just part of the *corredo da sposa* that the Principessa had firmly insisted on providing.

All of it far more glamorous than anything I'd have chosen for myself, she thought with a sigh, as she stretched out on the cushions, and, under the circumstances, a total waste of money.

As were the wages of this maid who'd been hired for her, of course, but she realised that this was an issue where it might be wiser to give way, as a nod in the direction of some kind of marital harmony.

After all I can't fight him about everything, she acknowledged dispiritedly. So I should save my ammunition for the battles that really matter. Whatever they turn out to be.

And found herself sighing again.

Angelo surveyed the information on his computer screen with tight-lipped satisfaction, and a certain relief. It seemed as if the finance deal with Credito Europa was going through without the last-minute hitches and prevarication that he had half-expected.

Apparently the Crocodile is a man of his word, after all, he thought cynically. And I, may God help me, am now married.

He pushed back his chair and stood up. He would have to return to Rome at some point to sign the necessary documentation, but that would not be a problem.

After all, his new bride was hardly likely to regret his absence, he thought coldly. *Al contrario*, having turned a once charming room into an efficient and characterless workspace as he'd recently observed, she would probably welcome his departure. See it as an opportunity to further the career that meant so much to her.

He wondered why the idea of her continuing to work for Avortino was irritating him so much. Surely he should welcome anything that would occupy her attention and keep her from enquiring too closely into his own activities.

And he should not have allowed his annoyance over her stubborn resistance to his wishes—or her apparent assumption that she was the only sufferer in their present situation—to get the better of him and goad him into inflicting on her that travesty of a kiss.

The holy saints knew it was the last thing he'd ever intended, he thought moodily. He'd planned to be kind and courteous, putting her at her ease in difficult circumstances, and instead he'd acted like the worst kind of boor.

His behaviour had been unbelievable, he told himself, besides creating an awkwardness between them that he knew he must somehow put right before it became unforgivable too.

Because, however rarely it might be, they were still committed to sharing a roof, and it would be helpful if they were able to do this with some degree of accord, even if it was only in public.

Mouth twisting, he took the Credito Europa's letter of confirmation from the printer. At least he could show her that there had already been some benefit from this unwanted marriage. That their mutual sacrifice was partially justified at least.

But it was by no means certain that he could persuade her to see it that way. He accepted ruefully now that it had been a serious error of judgement as well as unkind to describe her as 'a nonentity'. She had a mind and a will of her own, the little Elena, and, it was clear, no very high opinion of him either.

So perhaps it was time, he told himself wryly, that he tried to make amends of some kind. Establish at least a working relationship. And try to end this strange day on better terms than its beginning.

If that was possible, he added silently, and sighed.

Ellie was drifting in and out of a light sleep when she was disturbed by a firm rap at the bedroom door, followed by the sound of the door itself opening.

Pushing her hair back from her face, she lifted herself on to an elbow, expecting to see the threatened maid. But, instead, to her shock, it was Angelo who came striding briskly into the room.

'What are you doing here?' Ellie, hideously aware that she was in her underwear, looked round vainly for a rug or even a shawl to put round her shoulders as a cover-up. 'What do you want?'

He too looked taken aback, a tinge of colour emphasising the sculpted cheekbones as his dark gaze scanned her then hurriedly turned to the paper in his hand. 'I came to share some news with you.'

'Couldn't it have waited?' she asked tautly.

'Yes,' he acknowledged, mouth tightening. 'But I thought it would please you to know that Prince Damiano has today agreed the deal with Galantana, and therefore our days together can be considered as already numbered.'

'Oh,' she said. 'I—I see. Well, that's—good.'

'I imagined you would think so.' He paused. 'However, there is also another matter that perhaps we should discuss.'

'If it's about the maid you've hired for me,' Ellie said quickly, 'Assunta's already told me.'

'The maid?' His brows lifted. 'No, it concerns the other staff.' He hesitated. 'I learned just now that a celebration dinner is being prepared for us tonight. The *sala da pranzo* has been specially decorated with flowers, and the Manzini *calice* taken from its cabinet and cleaned. I should warn you that at some point in the evening, it will be filled with wine and various herbs and tradition demands that we drink from it while the household applaud.'

Ellie frowned. 'Is that a problem?'

'Not for me.' Angelo shrugged. 'But to share the *calice* will also signify our hope for a blissful wedding night and many babies to follow.' He gave her a sardonic look. 'It figures, therefore, that they will not expect us to sleep apart on such a meaningful occasion.'

Ellie sat up, embarrassment forgotten. She said crisply, 'Then they'll have to be disappointed.'

'You said in the car that you needed to gain their respect,' he reminded her softly. 'I must tell you, Elena, that to reveal yourself so soon as a wife who is no wife at all will not win that respect for you. *Infatti*, it could have the opposite effect.'

'That's a risk I'll just have to take.'

'Even when it could so easily be avoided?'

'You mean if I let you sleep with me?' She shook her head. Her voice sounded stifled. 'Never. Oh God, I knew I couldn't trust you.'

'I mean,' he said coldly, 'if I spend tonight in this room rather than my own. Nothing more.' He glanced around him. 'As you can see, it could easily accommodate half a dozen people.' He added more gently, 'Believe me, Elena *mia*, you would not wish them to think you displease me. Your life here will be much easier if it is thought we are truly man and wife, and that there is at least affection between us.'

She stared up at him. 'And you—being here tonight will be enough to convince them of that?'

'It will probably be necessary to pay you other visits in the future,' he said. 'But they will be few and I will make them brief. I shall not again stay all night.' His mouth twisted. 'If I wait until you are asleep, you will not even be aware of my presence.'

He watched her as she sat head bent, staring down at the floor. At last, she sighed.

'Yes, then—if I must. But you have to promise that you'll keep your word. That you won't try to—to...'

'The world is full of willing women, *mia cara*,' Angelo drawled, his voice faintly derisive. 'I have never forced my attentions on a reluctant girl yet. Believe me, you will not be the first.'

He paused. 'However, once we have drunk from the *calice* tonight, I shall be expected to kiss you. Perhaps, in return, you could smile at me? Is it agreed?'

As she nodded unwillingly, there was a tap on the door, and he turned. 'Ah, Donata.' He spoke pleasantly to the plump dark girl hesitating awkwardly in the doorway. 'The Contessa has been waiting to meet you, is that not so, *carissima*?' He took Ellie's hand and raised it fleetingly to his lips, adding huskily, 'Until later then, *mi amore*. I can hardly wait to be alone with you at last.'

And Ellie watched him go, in the furious knowledge that she was blushing to the roots of her hair.

Her day did not improve as it proceeded into evening.

Donata was polite and efficient, and sighed openly over the

handmade silk and lace underwear that she laid out for Ellie to put on after her bath, but at the same time there was just the faintest suggestion in her manner that her new employer probably needed all the help she could get.

Or am I being over-sensitive? Ellie asked herself drily.

Whatever, it made no real difference, she decided, shrugging mentally. She was not, as the maid clearly assumed, dressing to be undressed later by her bridegroom. Merely forcing herself to do what was expected of her.

Just as later in the *sala da pranzo*, she disguised her total lack of appetite by making herself eat at least some of all the delicious food set in front of her at a candle-lit table, garlanded with pink and white roses, and gleaming with silver and crystal.

And when the *calice* was ceremoniously borne in—beaten gold, no less, and engraved with the Manzini coat of arms—she rose, laughing, to her feet and stood in the circle of Angelo's arm as they drank, even managing to endure the firm, warm pressure of his mouth on hers when he bent to claim his kiss.

After which, as he had warned her, she was required to retire demurely to her room, and await her husband's pleasure.

'Are there any other embarrassing medieval customs I should know about?' she'd asked him stonily, aware that her skin was warming again. 'I hope they won't want to inspect the sheets to prove that I was a virgin.'

His mouth had hardened. 'And I hope there may come a time, Elena, when you may appreciate their pleasure in having you as their Contessa and respond more graciously.'

When she got to her room, the officious Donata had already been there to turn down the bed on both sides, and lay across its foot the faintly austere white satin nightgown and the matching robe, tying at the waist with ribbons in which Ellie was supposed to entrance her bridegroom, then, her duty done, had discreetly and thankfully departed.

Ellie hung away the pretty primrose dress she'd worn at dinner, put her discarded underwear in the clothes basket, and slid the slender length of satin over her head. As she turned to reach for the robe, she caught a momentary glimpse of herself in the long wall-mirror and paused, arrested, aware that for the first time that day she actually looked like a bride.

And found herself wondering suddenly what it would have been like if her marriage had been a real one to a man she loved and who loved her in return, so that she'd be waiting here with delight and anticipation for her husband to come to her and take her in his arms.

And was assailed by a wave of such bleak loneliness that she almost cried out in despair.

Biting her lip, she put on the robe, fastened it, then sat down at the dressing table and began to brush her hair with slow rhythmic strokes, in an attempt to restore herself to calm, so that she could meet Angelo's arrival with the necessary cool and unemotional indifference.

Or at least his eventual arrival, she thought when an hour had passed with no sign of him. She rose from the *chaise longue*, where she'd been perching nervously, retrieved the book she'd brought with her from the *palazzo*, a detective story set in Florence, removed her robe and, getting into bed, began to read.

Somewhere in the house, she heard a clock strike yet another hour and she paused, glancing at the door. Perhaps he'd changed his mind, she thought hopefully, having decided that their public performance with the loving cup was quite enough to fulfil the hopes of their well-wishers.

She closed her book and turned to switch off the lamp on her night table only to realise that her bedroom door was opening once again to admit Angelo. He came in quietly, and halted, looking at her across the room, brows raised quizzically.

He said, 'I thought by now you would indeed be asleep.'

He was wearing, she saw with a sudden thud of the heart, a black silk knee-length robe and apparently nothing else. And for a devastating moment, found herself remembering the night in the tower room and the touch of his bare skin against hers.

'I—I was reading,' she returned, her mouth suddenly dry.

'It must be a fascinating book to keep you awake until this

hour.' He began to walk slowly towards the bed. 'Perhaps you should lend it to me to provide me with a suitable diversion for the next week or so. Just as a precaution, you understand.'

He reached the other side of the bed and began to untie the sash that fastened his robe at the waist.

Ellie said hoarsely, 'What are you doing?'

'Getting ready to sleep, *naturalmente*. Or is that perhaps a *trabocchetto*—a trick question?'

'But you can't,' she protested. 'At least—not here.'

'If you imagine, *mia sposa*, that I intend to spend the night on that penance of a couch, then you are quite mistaken.'

'But it's perfectly comfortable.'

Angelo shrugged gracefully. 'For you, perhaps, for an hour during the siesta. Not for a man of my height at any time.'

'Then I'll sleep there myself,' she flared, pushing away the covers and swinging her legs out of the bed.

'And I prefer that you remain where you are.' He spoke quietly but there was a note of steel in his voice. 'I advise you to accede to my wishes in this, Elena. Do so, and we shall both pass a peaceful night. But to defy me and force me to bring you back to this bed might have consequences you would not care for.'

He paused. 'Now I suggest you turn your back, switch off the light and relax. You will soon forget that I am here.'

For a rigid, disquieting moment, she remained where she was, mentally weighing the possible repercussions of disobedience and realising reluctantly that she could not afford to take the risk.

Slowly she slid back under the covers and reached again for the lamp switch, plunging the room into darkness. As she did so, she felt the faint dip in the mattress signalling that he was now lying beside her, even if it was at a safe distance.

But there is no real safety, she thought, resting her hot cheek against the cool of the pillow. I'm in uncharted territory here, and I'm scared. As for forgetting that he's here—how impossible is that?

By contrast, however, Angelo seemed to have little difficulty in ignoring her presence. In a matter of minutes, or so it seemed to Ellie, his quiet even breathing revealed that he had fallen asleep, leaving her to lie awake and restive, but unable to show it, her only alternative to gaze unseeingly into the shadows, counting the long minutes as they turned slowly into hours and thinking of all the other nights ahead of her when she would have to do the same, until the time when this strange—even incredible—non-marriage finally came to its end.

And hoping, with something approaching desperation, that it might be soon.

Three months later

Ellie closed her laptop, and stretched gently, easing her back. At the same time, she allowed herself a faint smile of satisfaction. Because of a colleague's illness, she'd just completed the translation of a lengthy scientific handbook, crammed with the kind of technical jargon known only to the initiated.

The inherent difficulty of the task, too, had demanded total concentration, which meant that she had less time to focus on other, more personal problems. Such as the equally inherent difficulty of presenting a convincing performance to the world in her ongoing role as the young Contessa Manzini, she thought unhappily.

Something which was preying on her mind more and more as her marriage began to turn from weeks into months, although she was at a loss to know why.

On the face of it, she had little to complain about. As she'd suspected it had not taken her long to become familiar with the household routine, which ran like clockwork anyway without any real intervention from her.

And, she had to admit, Angelo had scrupulously kept his word as to how their lives together would be conducted, which was quite simply—apart. That since their wedding night, he had paid precisely three visits to her room, and those only for the sake of appearances, during which they'd slept on strictly opposite sides of that gigantic bed.

And he had never even attempted to lay a hand on her.

Not that she wanted him to, of course, she reminded herself swiftly. So, it was a relief to know that he clearly shared—maybe even exceeded—her own reluctance.

Because there had been no repetition of that burning savagery of a kiss either. His greeting and leave-taking invariably consisted of the merest brush of his lips across her cheek and her fingers, and that only when others were present.

And if there were moments when she wondered whether the marriage was setting a pattern and that she was destined to spend the rest of her life alone and undesired, she kept such thoughts strictly to herself, pretending that the possibility was not as hurtful as it sometimes felt.

And that, of course, there would be someone—someday—when this was over and life became real again.

So there was really nothing for her to be uneasy about. Or not where Angelo was concerned, anyway, she amended swiftly.

Because she could not deny she was being subjected to pressure of a different nature and from another source entirely. Something she had never expected, and found increasingly difficult to deal with.

She got up from her seat and walked restlessly over to the window, staring out at the sunlit landscape with eyes that pictured another scene entirely.

It had begun some six weeks after the wedding. Her godmother had invited her to a lunch party at Largossa—'A very small affair, *mia cara*, and all female.'

She'd been delighted to find Nonna Cosima present, but less pleased to see Signora Luccino, whom she was learning to call Zia Dorotea. For some reason, the older woman had seemed convinced from the start that Ellie's marriage was entirely her own design, and that she deserved the credit for bringing it about.

And how wrong was it possible for anyone to be? Ellie thought bitterly. But at least the Signora had brought Tullia with her, which promised some alleviation.

It was during the *aperitivos* before lunch that the first blow fell.

'You look well, *cara* Elena,' Zia Dorotea pronounced magisterially. 'Almost blooming, in fact. Is it possible you have good news for us all?'

Ellie set down her glass of *prosecco* with immense care, controlling the silent scream building inside her. She was aware of Madrina and Nonna Cosima exchanging glances of faint anguish and Tullia's open glare at her mother, but it made no difference. The words had been spoken. The question 'Are you pregnant?' was out there, and awaiting an answer.

Only she had none to give.

She forced a smile. 'I spent the weekend at Porto Vecchio. If I have colour in my cheeks, it's probably thanks to the sun and sea breezes.'

'I hope Angelo has also benefited from the break,' said Signora Luccino. 'The last time I saw him, I thought he looked a little strained.'

Ellie bit her lip. 'He wasn't able to accompany me. He had—engagements.' *And please don't ask me where or with whom because I didn't ask him, and I don't want to know anyway.*

'Besides,' she added. 'It wouldn't be his kind of place. It's altogether—too basic.'

'You are saying he has never been there?' The Signora sounded scandalised. 'That you go alone when you have been married less than two months?'

'Oh, Mamma,' Tullia intervened impatiently. 'Husbands and wives do not have to live in each other's pockets.'

'Then perhaps they should,' was the austere reply. 'Particularly when the future of an ancient dynasty is involved. Angelo needs an heir, and perhaps he should be reminded of the fact.'

Nonna Cosima intervened gently. 'I think, my dear Dorotea, that we should allow the children to conduct their own lives, and enjoy the freedom of these first months of marriage together. I am sure the nurseries at Vostranto will be occupied soon enough.'

'But hardly when Angelo spends all week in Rome and Elena disappears to the coast without him at weekends,' the Signora returned implacably. 'I gave birth to my own son within the first year of my marriage, because I knew what my duty was.'

Ellie looked down at the gleam of her wedding ring, her face wooden, thankful that no-one in the room knew the entire truth about her relationship with her supposed husband.

At which point, Giovanni had arrived to announce that the Principessa was served, and Ellie was off the hook.

But not permanently, of course. Ever since there'd been little hints, little nudges, often growing into far more pointed enquiries about her health each time she encountered the Signora.

If things had been different with Angelo, she thought, if they'd been something approaching friends instead of strangers whose paths occasionally crossed, then she could have mentioned it to him—perhaps made a joke of it—but asking for it to stop at the same time.

As it was, she had to endure in a silence that was actually becoming painful in some strange way.

Now, she found she was watching her reflection in the glass panes, studying without pleasure the set of her mouth and the guarded wary eyes. If she'd ever bloomed, she thought with a sigh, there were few signs of that now.

She was startled to hear the distant clang of the bell at the front door. Visitors at Vostranto were rare during the week, and did not usually call without an appointment or an invitation. Perhaps the caller had come to the wrong house, she thought.

Yet a few moments later, there was a tap on the door heralding Giorgio's arrival.

'The Signora Alberoni has called, madam. I have shown her into the *salotto*.'

For a moment she stared at him, initial incomprehension turning into disbelief. Silvia—*Silvia* here? It wasn't possible.

'No, I won't see her. Tell her to go.'

The angry impetuous denial was so clear in her head that she thought she'd already spoken it aloud, until she realised

Giorgio was still waiting for her reply, his expression faintly surprised. Her hands had balled into fists in the folds of her denim skirt and she made herself unclench them, forcing a smile.

'*Grazie*, Giorgio. Will you please ask Assunta to bring coffee and some of the little raisin biscuits? And perhaps Bernardina has made some almond cake?'

Going through the motions of hospitality, she thought, when what she really wanted was to run away screaming.

Then, mustering her composure, she walked down the hall to the *salotto* to confront the cousin who, in one tumultuous night, had brought about the ruin of her life.

CHAPTER SEVEN

ONE LOOK AT Silvia told Ellie that her cousin was not there to
apologise. She was standing in the centre of the room, a dark
red silk dress clinging to every curve, her eyes narrowed as
she surveyed her surroundings.

'You've done well for yourself, *cara*,' she commented, send-
ing Ellie's elderly skirt and collarless white blouse a derisive
look. 'Strange how things sometimes turn out.'

She walked over to the fireplace and studied the coat of
arms carved into its stonework. 'This is the first time I have
been here. Did you know that?'

'No,' Ellie returned quietly. 'I didn't know.'

Silvia tossed her head, making her blonde hair shimmer.
'I tried several times to persuade Angelo to invite me, but he
always made some excuse.'

'I see.' Ellie lifted her chin. 'So, what excuse do you have
for making this visit now?'

Silvia spread her hands gracefully. 'Do I need one—to see
my own cousin?' She paused. 'I didn't send you a wedding
present, because what can one possibly give someone who's
scooped the equivalent of the Euro-lottery? It was really very
clever of you.'

She walked to a sofa and sat down crossing her legs. 'Or
was it?' Her tone was meditative. 'Maybe it was all the idea of
that old witch, his grandmother and her daughter, the Luccino
woman. God knows that precious pair have been trying to force

him into an unwanted marriage for years. Did I supply them with the chance they wanted?'

She laughed harshly. 'How ironic. How truly ironic.'

Ellie took a step forward. 'Silvia—how could you do such a thing?'

'Why wouldn't I?' Silvia's eyes flashed. 'Did he think—did he really think that I would allow him to throw me aside as if I was nothing? No-one treats me like that—ever. I knew the importance of his deal with Zio Cesare and how damaging its failure would be. Therefore, I decided to teach him a lesson.' Her smile was calculating. 'I knew I could still make him want me, and that he would not be able to resist my invitation.'

Ellie said in a low voice, 'I meant—how could you involve me? As you've just said—your own cousin.'

Silvia shrugged negligently. 'Because I knew you were the last girl in the world that Angelo would ever find attractive, so that when he was found in your room, he would look and feel a complete fool. It was the final perfect touch.'

Ellie turned away. She said in a stifled voice, 'You must be mad.'

'He made me suffer,' Silvia retorted. 'I wanted him to suffer too. To realise what he had lost when he ended our affair.'

'But it couldn't have continued,' Ellie protested. 'What would have happened if Ernesto had found out?'

Her cousin shrugged again. 'He would have divorced me, *naturalmente*, and I would have been free to marry Angelo, who must now be wishing every day of his life that he had not been so hasty and thrown away our happiness.'

Happiness? thought Ellie with disbelief. What happiness could possibly grow from such a selfish obsession—or from inflicting misery on others?

She took a deep breath. 'If that's all you came to say, maybe you should leave.'

'When I'm enjoying all this fabulous hospitality?' Silvia gave a little, tinkling laugh. 'I think I'll stay for a while so we can chat—woman to woman.' Her voice sank intimately. 'I'm dying to know, *carissima*, how you like married life. Does Angelo fulfil every lonely little fantasy you ever had?'

Her gaze swept mockingly over Ellie's shrinking body. 'I must tell you that you do not seem the picture of rapture, *mia cara*.'

'You can think what you wish.' Ellie lifted her chin. 'However, I have no intention of discussing my relationship with…' She hesitated. She could not bring herself to say 'Angelo' because she never used his given name. On the other hand she could hardly say, 'Count Manzini' to Silvia of all people.

So she compromised with 'my husband'—a description totally lacking in accuracy, too, she reminded herself with a faint stab of unexpected pain.

Although she'd always known that she would have to see her cousin again one day, she'd imagined an occasion when others would be present, obliging her to find a way to smile, be civil and pass on.

She had not bargained for this one-to-one confrontation, or that it would take place so soon—or here—on territory that should have been taboo.

She was surprised that the Count had not given private orders that Signora Alberoni was not to be admitted, but perhaps he'd not believed she would have the gall to simply—invite herself like this.

She was thankful that he was not returning to Vostranto until the following evening. She could only imagine his reaction if he'd arrived back to find his former mistress comfortably ensconced in his *salotto*.

That unaccountable pain stirred inside her again. She'd tried very hard not to think about Angelo and Silvia as lovers, but the gloating expression in her cousin's eyes had said more loudly than any words that she hadn't forgotten a thing about sharing his bed and his body.

That Silvia was able to recall all the kind of intensely intimate details about him—how it felt to be kissed by him, touched, taken in passion—that Ellie would never know.

That she didn't want to know, she corrected herself hastily, but which put her at a terrible disadvantage just the same.

She was aware too that she wasn't handling the situation particularly well, and that Silvia would be enjoying her discomfiture.

And the knowledge that Angelo had never brought his former mistress here in spite of some pretty heavy-duty wheedling was somehow very little comfort.

It was almost a relief when a tap on the door heralded the arrival of Assunta, with a maid following her, pushing a trolley laden with coffee and a lavish selection of biscuits, cakes and pastries.

'*Dio mio.*' Silvia's laugh sounded melodiously again. 'But how delicious! I am being so spoiled today.'

But you always have been, Ellie wanted to say. From birth, according to Nonna Vittoria. The baby visited in your cradle only by good fairies bringing you beauty, charm and uncritical love from all those around you. Making you believe that you could have anything you wanted, and live for yourself alone. And that, whatever you did, you would be forgiven.

And I signed up to that too, went along with it for all these years, even though Nonna—and later Madrina—tried to warn me gently to be careful. Because, even if I was always on your side, there was no guarantee you'd always be on mine. Why couldn't I see that?

Maybe that was why Nonna bequeathed the house at Porto Vecchio to me—because she knew that, some day, something you'd do would make me need a refuge.

Aloud, she said quietly, 'Assunta, please make sure that the Signora's driver is looked after.'

'Oh, I drove myself, *cara*,' Silvia informed her, shrugging. 'As I often do these days.' She turned a brilliant smile on the housekeeper. 'So you are the wonderful Assunta. Count Manzini has sung your praises to me so often.'

Assunta inclined her head in a manner that managed to be polite and sceptical at the same time, then withdrew leaving the maid Rosaria to pour the coffee into the exquisite bone china cups, and hand round the plates of delicacies, giving Silvia the opportunity to fuss with wistful sweetness over the calorific content of each offering.

'I have to be so careful of my figure for *caro* Ernesto's sake,' she sighed. 'A woman owes it to her husband to make the best of herself, don't you think so, Elena *mia*?' A comment which accompanied another disparaging look at what Ellie was wearing, and also took in the fact that her hair was drawn back and crammed into an elastic band at the nape of her neck.

I don't think Angelo would care particularly if I starved myself to death or ate until I burst, she thought, suppressing a silent sigh, and deliberately selecting a choux pastry oozing cream.

Even when Rosaria left and they were alone, there were thankfully no further inroads into the subject of Ellie's marriage, and Silvia reverted to talking about herself—parties she had attended, film premieres where she had been a guest, a fabulous new boutique, a miraculous new hairdresser.

'Such a pity you do not spend more time in Rome, *cara*. I could show you a whole new world.' Silvia delicately wiped some crumbs of almond cake from her fingertips and put down the linen napkin. 'But for now you can show me your world,' she added, a little smile playing around her lips. 'So—the full guided tour, if you please.' And paused before adding, 'Including, of course, the bedrooms.'

Ellie replaced her cup carefully on its saucer, swallowing down the silent scream rising inside her.

She said levelly, 'I'll ring for Assunta. She knows far more about the house's history than I do.'

Silvia pouted. 'If you wish, but I would rather hear it from you, the mistress of all this magnificence. And of its master, too.' She shook her head, as she rose, smoothing her dress over her hips with a languid gesture. 'Ella-Bella, the little mouse. Who would ever believe it?'

Well, I wouldn't for one, Ellie thought as she crossed the room and tugged at the embroidered bell pull beside the wide hearth. Because I know it couldn't be further from the truth. And so, I suspect, does she.

And wondered again why Silvia was there.

He still could not believe what he had done. It was ridiculous—impossible—almost making him doubt his own sanity.

Because all the arrangements had been in place. The carefully chosen flowers delivered that morning. The lunch reservation in the eminent restaurant of an exclusive hotel, with coffee served privately and discreetly in a suite on the first floor when the meal was over.

And he had talked to her and smiled, and let his eyes caress her, watching her lips part on a small indrawn breath as the first flush of overt desire warmed her smooth skin.

Beautiful, sexy and much more than willing, he'd thought pleasurably. Exactly the kind of recreation he needed after the long hours he'd been working to finalise the Galantana project, and a glorious end to the past weeks of celibacy.

Even now he couldn't be sure of the moment when it first occurred to him that it was not going to happen. Wasn't aware of having made the decision, or why he'd done so. He only knew, without a shadow of doubt, that when lunch concluded, there would be no delicious consummation between silk sheets, accompanied by five star brandy. That, in fact, he would be making an excuse and leaving. Regretfully, *naturalmente*, but quite definitely.

He'd seen her shock, her disbelief as she realised the promised seduction was not going to happen after all, then pride had come swiftly to her rescue—and to his. Even so, he'd gone out into the heat of the afternoon calling himself every kind of bastard.

He'd told his secretary that he would not be back in his office that day, so a return to his apartment seemed the obvious choice. And possibly a cold shower, he'd thought in self-derision.

Yet, for some reason, here he was, driving towards Vostranto.

Now I know I'm crazy, he thought bitterly. Because what kind of a welcome can I expect there?

He pulled the car over on to the verge, switching off the engine and staring ahead through the windscreen, his dark eyes moody. The image of a girl's face rose up in front of him, pale and strained, her soft mouth unsmiling, her eyes sliding nervously away from his. It had been the same each time they'd been together since the wedding, and the truth was that he was at a total loss to know how to ease the unhappy situation between them.

She was, he told himself, unreachable. At least by him. Not, of course, that he had wanted to reach her, he reminded himself swiftly. Not at the beginning when he'd dismissed her so contemptuously as a potential bride.

He'd soon realised, however, that his description of her as a nonentity had been unfair and unjustified. That she'd quickly demonstrated that she had a mind—and a will—all her own which she was prepared to pit against his.

Now, for the first time, he found himself wondering if there'd perhaps been someone else in her life. If his unwelcome intrusion had actually robbed her of a lover, for whom she was still grieving, and if that was why she continued to shrink from him—particularly on those few nightmare occasions when they shared a bed, and she lay a few feet away from him in a trembling silence that had nothing to do with sleep.

But no, he decided, his mouth twisting. If Elena had been in love, had given herself to another man, she would not have been considered by Zia Dorotea or his grandmother as a suitable candidate to become the Contessa Manzini. Which, for some unfathomable reason, she undoubtedly had been, long before Silvia Alberoni's machinations had forced them together so ludicrously.

Leaving him stranded in the unenviable position of being a husband but without a wife.

Although she was hardly to blame for that, he thought ruefully. In the time leading up to the wedding had he made any real attempt to woo her? To alleviate for her the humiliation of knowing that she was being married only to preserve a business deal and persuade her instead that, even if they could not expect marital bliss, they might achieve a working relationship with perhaps some attendant pleasure?

Then proved it by stealing her away from the *palazzo* and coaxing her somehow into letting him make gentle lingering love to her.

Yet, in reality, furious at being manipulated into such a proposal, he had instead stressed that their union was a strictly temporary arrangement which would be dispensed with swiftly and efficiently at the appropriate time. And that there would be no physical intimacy between them.

That was what he'd promised, and what, it seemed, he now had to live with.

Because there seemed little chance of any alteration in the *status quo*, he thought flatly. Indeed, the available evidence suggested that she was not even marginally attracted to him. That she might even dislike him or, which was worse, fear being alone with him.

It should never have come to this, he told himself bleakly. I should not have allowed it to happen. And I cannot let it go on.

With an abrupt sigh, he re-started the car and pulled out on to the road.

As he approached the next long bend, he heard the sound of another vehicle's horn, blowing in warning, and, with that, a lorry came round the corner in the act of being overtaken by a dark blue Maserati.

Angelo was already braking, his mind filled with a confused impression of the lorry driver's white face and a fist being shaken, as he swerved, swiftly and urgently, hearing the crunch of metal as his wing made glancing contact with a concrete block lying in the grass at the side of the road.

He stopped a few yards further on, and sat for a moment aware that he was shaking, his heart going like a trip-hammer. He'd had near misses before, but that was the closest he'd ever come to total disaster.

Santa Madonna, he thought. If I'd been doing any real speed...

He saw that the lorry had also come to a halt, and the driver and another man were running back to him.

The Maserati, however, had vanished.

As if on auto-pilot, he assured his anxious questioners that he was not injured, and that the damage to his car was slight. An annoyance only that could have been so much worse.

'And I did not even get the number of the car, *signore*.' The lorry driver shook his head in disbelief as he prepared to depart. *'Dio mio,'* he added from the heart. 'Women drivers!'

'Yes,' Angelo returned softly and grimly. 'Women drivers.'

Because he had recognised the car, so he already knew its number, and who had been at the wheel, and cold, burning anger was building inexorably inside him as he resumed his journey towards Vostranto, as well as a sense of grim determination.

Ellie watched Giorgio close the massive door, and listened with a sense of almost overwhelming relief as the car roared away down the drive, taking her unwanted guest away at last.

Feeling as if she'd been wrung out, mentally and emotionally, she turned to the major domo. 'I have a slight headache, Giorgio. I'm going to rest for a while.'

She refused his concerned offers of tea, painkillers or a cold compress for the forehead, and returned upstairs to the room she'd left only a few minutes before.

It hadn't changed in any material sense, but it was different all the same. Silvia still seemed to be there, scrutinising everything, insisting on seeing even the bathroom and the dressing room, where her eyes had narrowed at the display of clothes on the hanging rails.

'At least you will look the part in public, *cara*, if he ever allows you to be seen there with him,' had been the first comment to grate across Ellie's nerve endings.

No detail seemed too small to be spared a remark.

But the focus of her attention had been the bed. She'd stood, unmoving, staring at it in silence, a smile playing about her full lips until Ellie had wanted to scream.

She'd said at last, 'I am trying to imagine you in the act of surrender on this bed, but strangely I find it quite impossible. You still look so innocent—so sadly untouched, it makes me wonder if he has ever taken the trouble to consummate the marriage. He will have to do so eventually, *naturalmente*,' she continued musingly. 'It is his duty to his family to have a son, as I am sure Contessa Cosima has told him, so you can be of use for that, if nothing else. I wonder what has been holding him back? Maybe he still thinks of what might have been—with me.'

Ellie forced herself to meet Silvia's mocking gaze. To speak levelly, 'Why don't you ask him?'

The smile widened, and became laughter. 'I shall not have to, Elena *mia*. He will tell me himself soon enough.'

She'd gone to the door, then suddenly paused and walked back, bending to run a caressing hand across the magnificence of the bedcover.

Her voice had been quiet but very distinct. 'It isn't over yet, *cara*. You have to understand that. Because I still want him. And I shall have him, just as I would have done that night. Except he had to be punished. But now I think he has suffered enough—don't you?'

And she had smiled again and left, hips swaying in her red dress, her hair a golden coronet in the late afternoon sun, while Ellie followed, numb with disbelief and some other emotions not quite so easily defined.

Now looking at the bed, seeing again Silvia's possessive fingers stroking its cover as if they were someone's skin, she felt as if she'd been somehow coated in slime. And, for a moment, terribly afraid—as if the sun had gone out forever, leaving her in darkness.

Oh come on, she adjured herself impatiently. You've just had an unpleasant hour or so, and it's thrown you because your own cousin's become someone you only thought you knew.

But for the moment at least, she found she did not want to lie down on the bed, and having tried and failed to get comfortable on the *chaise longue*, she decided to attempt a different ploy.

She walked into the bathroom, shedding her clothes as she went, and turned on the shower, gratefully allowing its powerful cascade to stream over her, washing away the foam from the scented gel she'd applied to her skin and with it some of the tensions and sense of unease left in Silvia's wake. And, if she was honest, some of the pain too.

Some, but not all, she thought as she stepped dripping out of the cubicle, reaching blindly for a towel.

Only to find herself being firmly enveloped in a bath sheet, then carried, swaddled and helpless, back into the bedroom where she was set on her feet.

'*Buona sera*, my sweet wife,' Angelo said softly. 'Does a shower cure a headache? I did not know that.'

Her lashes felt gummed together by the water, but she prised them open somehow staring up at him with mingled anger and shock.

'What are you doing here?' she demanded breathlessly, stepping back and trying not to trip on the trailing bath sheet. Trying, too, not to blush and failing miserably. 'How dare you—walk in on me like that?'

The sculpted mouth curled. 'And how dare you invite your *sciattona* of a cousin here in my absence?' he retorted coldly. 'Did you think I would welcome such a guest—or simply hope I would not find out? I am waiting to hear.'

She'd had a rotten afternoon and now this—this hideous embarrassment of knowing he'd seen her naked for a second time. She longed for the floor to open and swallow her, but it was clearly not going to do so, so she lifted her chin defiantly. 'I do not have to explain myself to you, *signore*.'

'Think again,' he invited crisply.

'Most of your family have visited us here.' She was hardly able to believe she was saying these things. That she was being such an idiot. Almost as stupid, she thought mutinously, as he was arrogant. What right had he to—turn up out of the blue like this and challenge her? 'Am I not allowed to see my only living relative in return?'

'I am astonished you should wish to do so.' The dark gaze narrowed. 'Or do you have more in common than I thought? Did the pair of you perhaps work together to fool us all that night at Largossa?'

She wanted to slap him hard across the face for that, but her arms were confined inside her wrapping, and she dared not try to free them in case the beastly towel slipped or fell off altogether.

'Believe whatever you want,' she snapped. 'It makes no difference to me. Now will you please go and allow me some privacy.'

'Privacy?' Angelo queried derisively. '*Santa Madonna*, what has there ever been in this marriage but privacy?'

She stiffened defensively. 'I'm sorry if you're not satisfied with your bargain.'

'And you are?' He looked her over in such a way that the sheltering towel seemed, disturbingly, no longer to exist. 'Perhaps I no longer believe that.'

'As I said before—think what you wish.' She was beginning to shiver in the damp folds, and did not want him to conclude that she was trembling. That she feared him in any way.

But—there was something different about him today. His unannounced arrival in her room was not the kind of aloof, courteous behaviour to which she'd become accustomed. Besides, his whole attitude seemed edgy—challenging, and this change in him bewildered her. Made her—anxious.

She added in a low voice, 'Angelo—please go.'

'When I am ready,' he said. 'Also when you have told me the truth about your cousin. Why was she here? What did she want?'

The bald answer to that was—'You,' but Ellie hesitated to return it, instinct telling her that these were dangerous waters when she was already out of her depth.

She said quietly, 'She wished to see the house. And, of course, to laugh at me.'

Oh God, she thought, I didn't intend to say that.

His gaze sharpened. 'For what reason?'

She swallowed. 'Because I'm completely out of place here. And everyone must know this.'

He said slowly, 'Elena, you are the Contessa Manzini. There is not a soul beneath this roof who does not regard you with affection and respect.'

Except yourself...

Dismissing the thought, Ellie bent her head. 'How can you say that when they know—they all must know that we're only pretending to be married.' *And Silvia in particular...*

'Forgive me, but I did not think you would be concerned.' His voice was level. '*Dopo tutto*, you have never given that impression.'

She stared at the floor. 'Perhaps it was today—seeing Silvia here—looking again at the portraits of the previous Contessas in the *salotto* and the dining room and seeing how beautiful they were, just as she is.' She added bitterly, 'How they would all have known how to behave—what was expected of them all the time—instead of being a fish out of water like me.'

The hardness of his mouth relaxed a little, and he spoke more gently. 'Elena, let me assure you that you do not resemble any fish known to the mind of man.'

'I'm being serious!'

'I am glad to hear it, because it is time we spoke seriously.'

She still didn't look at him. She said with faint breathlessness, 'Is that why you're suddenly here in the middle of the week—to tell me that you've decided to end the marriage?'

For a brief instant, Angelo was sorely tempted to tell her the whole truth—that he'd been on the brink of spending an enjoyable afternoon in bed with a beautiful girl he'd met at a dinner party two nights earlier, but had suddenly changed his mind for reasons he could not explain even to himself.

That he'd decided to return home on another apparent whim, but that the incident on the road which could so easily have left him seriously injured or dead had turned an impulse into resolution.

Which now prompted him to offer her honesty along with the new beginning which had now crystallised in his mind.

Starting with the moment he had seen her standing naked in the shower, the tendrils of soaked hair hanging round her face, the droplets of water running down over the pale skin of her breasts to her midriff and the slight concavity of her belly, and glistening on her slender thighs.

Recalling too how his body had stirred under his sudden sharp desire to lick each tiny trickle from her flesh and watch her rosy nipples lift and firm to hard peaks under the glide of his tongue.

Had he forgotten, he wondered in astonishment, or had he simply not noticed on that far off night just how lovely she looked without clothing?

Then paused, just in time as he realised the exact nature of his prospective confession.

'*Sciocco*,' he apostrophised himself silently. '*Idiota*.'

Dio mio, his near-miss must have affected his brain if he imagined for one moment that might be what she wanted to hear from him.

No, he thought, it would be far better—wiser to use the opportunity she had given him, and, leaving all other issues aside, start by answering the question she had asked.

'No,' he said quietly. 'That is not why I am here. *Al contrario*.'

She looked up at that, her eyes widening, but, he thought, in apprehension more than pleasure, and took a swift mental step backwards.

He went on, 'I regret if my displeasure at your cousin's visit caused me to speak roughly to you.'

'It doesn't matter.' The grey-green eyes slid past him as if she was looking at the bed. 'Although you couldn't possibly imagine I would actually invite her here.'

'Perhaps, *mia bella*, I was not thinking too clearly. But I am a little more lucid now, and I have a proposition to put to you.'

He paused. 'Elena, I would like you to reconsider the terms of our marriage.'

She repeated 'Reconsider?' as if she had never heard the word before. Then: 'In what way—reconsider?'

'You said earlier that the other Contessas knew what was expected of them, and that is true. They were aware, *per esempio*, that a priority in their lives was to provide an heir for the Manzini dynasty, to ensure our ancient name did not die.'

She did not move. It was as if, he thought, she'd been turned to stone inside the towel that swathed her.

'And I have the same wish—the same dream of a son to follow me. I am asking you, therefore, to make our marriage a real one. To live with me as my wife, and become, in time, the mother of my child.'

She stared at him, lips parted, her gaze almost blank and he continued hurriedly, 'I do not require you to answer me now, Elena. I realise you need time to think.' He paused. 'I hope we can discuss the matter later—over dinner *forse*.'

He smiled at her swiftly and, he hoped, reassuringly, then turned and walked to the door.

Ellie watched him go, with a sense of total unreality, as Silvia's mocking words buzzed in her head. *'His duty to his family to have a son,'* her cousin had said. And *'You can be of use for that, if nothing else...'*

This is crazy, she thought. It cannot be happening to me. I must be having a bad dream while I'm sleeping off my headache.

And even if it was all true—if he'd really been here asking her to change her entire life, her hopes for the future—her answer, now and for all time, was 'No.'

What else could it possibly be? she asked herself. And felt tears, harsh and wholly unexpected, burn suddenly in her throat and blur her startled eyes.

CHAPTER EIGHT

WHEN SHE WAS calm again, Ellie washed the tearstains from her face, dried her hair, placed her discarded clothing in the linen basket, and put on her robe.

As she tied its sash, her attention was attracted by the noise of some heavy vehicle in the courtyard below. When she went to the window, she was surprised to see Angelo's car being loaded on the back of a transporter. As the truck departed with its load, there was a rap on the door, and Assunta entered carrying a pile of clean towels.

Ellie turned. 'Is there something wrong with the *signore*'s car, Assunta?'

The older woman stared at her, astonished. 'But it was damaged in the accident, Contessa. You must know that.'

'Accident?' Ellie queried, startled. 'I—I don't think I understand.'

Assunta shook her head. 'There was nearly a collision with another car overtaking when it should not have done so.' She crossed herself. 'The *signore* escaped without injury, may God be praised, through his own swift action. Otherwise he might have been killed.' She paused. 'Did he not tell you this?'

'No,' Ellie said slowly. 'He—didn't mention it.'

'Perhaps he did not wish to cause you concern.' Assunta's warm, inquisitive gaze scanned Ellie's slim figure, as if seeking for a reason for the Count to show such consideration to his young wife.

'Yes,' Ellie agreed quietly. 'Perhaps.'

'The Count wishes me to say that dinner will be served at eight o'clock this evening,' Assunta continued. 'After his ordeal, he will need an early night, *senza dubbio*.'

'*Sì*,' Ellie said after a pause. 'No doubt he will.'

When Assunta had delivered her towels to the bathroom and left, Ellie wandered back to the *chaise longue* and sat down, staring into space.

He might have been killed...

An uncontrollable shiver ran through her. Yes, she'd have had the promised freedom but at what kind of terrible cost? Didn't they say—Be careful what you wish for, because it could be granted?

She suddenly had an image of him standing in front of her, as he had been so short a time before. Could see the lean, long-legged body, his powerful shoulders undisguised by his elegant suit, the dark incisive face, the fathomless eyes and the swift, slanting smile as if they'd been etched on her brain.

Was aware of a tug of something which was almost like yearning, secret and unbidden, and which she had never experienced before. And could not afford to experience again.

A real marriage...

His words seemed to take on the impact of a siren song, with the power to beckon her to disaster, and she knew she could not allow that to happen.

He had married her from necessity not desire, and necessity was still driving him. It would be futile and dangerous to think otherwise.

At the same time, maybe she should re-think the bluntly negative response she'd been planning. Find some other way to tell him what he asked was impossible.

Silvia had said that she could not imagine her surrendering to Angelo on that bed. Well, she could not do so either. Could not, she told herself as her heart thundered against her ribcage. And would not.

Or not in the way he would undoubtedly have in mind.

Because she was simply a matter of expediency to him—as she always had been and always would be. And having his baby would be no different either. She would be little more than a surrogate mother. Stories in the papers suggested that women were well paid to use their bodies for such a purpose, but under strict terms and conditions.

She could formulate her own, she told herself. Rules to be strictly observed which would also safeguard her against harbouring any absurd fantasies about him, or about her role in his life.

And the price of her compliance would be her eventual escape from this meaningless existence that had been forced on her and the regaining of her freedom. That would be made totally clear.

For a moment, she quailed inwardly at the prospect of telling him, then rose, squaring her shoulders. After all, she thought, as long as he gets the heir he wants, why should he care? It may even be a relief.

She waited until it was almost eight o'clock before she ventured downstairs. To Donata's obvious disapproval, she'd insisted on wearing her plainest dress, a simple crossover style in white silk, and left her hair loose.

She found Angelo standing by the open windows in the *salotto*, looking broodingly over the gardens, a glass of his usual whisky in his hand. He turned as she entered, his brows lifting. '*Mia bella,*' he said softly. 'You look like a bride again.'

Ellie was taken aback. She'd meant to indicate that she hadn't taken any particular trouble with her appearance. That, for her, this was just—any evening. She said with constraint, 'That was not my intention.'

He clicked his tongue, his smile glinting. 'You disappoint me. Would you like a drink?'

'*Sì, grazie.* Some fresh orange juice.'

'You do not think the circumstances call for something stronger?' He added ice to the tumbler and brought it to her.

She took the drink with a word of thanks. 'I suppose you mean the circumstances of my learning from Assunta that you'd apparently escaped death by inches?' She kept her voice cool and level.

'*Si*—among other things.'

The juice was sweet and refreshingly cold against her dry throat. 'Is that why you suddenly decided you needed a child to carry on your name? Why you no longer wanted to wait for the day when you'd be rid of me at last and able to find a wife more to your taste?'

His tone was reflective. 'It reminded me, *certamente*, how unexpected life can become—and how fragile. And that it is by no means certain that the future Contessa you describe even exists.'

'But you'll never know,' she said. 'Unless you try to find her.'

'Ah,' Angelo said softly. 'But that could take forever, and I also realised how unwise it is to allow time to—waste.' He paused. 'Besides, my decision was not as sudden as you may think.'

She said huskily, 'And if I say I still find it—unacceptable.'

'Then I shall try to persuade you to change your mind. I have not forgotten, *carissima*, how sweet your lips once tasted.' His gaze travelled slowly from her mouth down to the slender curves now hidden by the discreet vee of her neckline. 'I believe, with your permission, that I could make you happy.'

'A practical demonstration of your famed skill with women?' Ellie lifted her chin. 'I don't think so.'

There was another silence, then he said, 'I would not have described my intentions in those terms.'

'Then we must agree to differ. In any case, it hardly matters.' She took a deep breath. 'The truth is you wish me to have your child. We do not have to be—lovers in the usual sense to achieve this.'

He said, frowning, 'Perhaps I sustained some blow on the head this afternoon, for I find myself singularly stupid tonight. Have the goodness to explain what you mean, *per favore*.'

'You told me earlier you wished me to—live with you—as your wife.' She stared down at the melting ice in her glass.

'But I—I wouldn't find that acceptable. However, if you simply wanted to change the manner of your—visits to me at night in order to make me pregnant, I would agree to that. But only that.'

There was a further, more ominous silence, then Angelo said quietly and courteously, 'I am still not sure I understand you. At least,' he corrected himself, 'I hope I do not. Are you saying, *effettivamente*, that you will allow me occasional access to your body solely for the purpose of procreation?'

'Yes.' She did not look at him.

He said hoarsely, '*Santa Madonna*, Elena, you surely cannot mean that.'

'I do mean it,' she said. 'Those are my conditions for having your child, and ensuring the Manzini succession. They won't change.'

He took a step closer, his hand reaching out as if to stroke her cheek, and Ellie recoiled, her heart skipping a beat as she retreated a step. He must believe, she thought, that he would only have to touch her...

Angelo halted, the dark brows snapping together as he studied her. He said at last, 'So am I never to hope that we will spend our nights sharing a bed together—sleeping in each other's arms after we have made love?'

She bit down on her lip. 'Why not hope instead, *signore*, that I waste none of the time you mentioned, and give you a son very quickly.' She paused. 'And I'm quite sure your nights won't be lonely without me, so you could be getting the best of both worlds.'

'How curious you should think so.' He drank the remainder of his whisky with an angry jerk of the arm, then walked to the door, holding it open for her with exaggerated politeness. 'And now, my dear wife, shall we have dinner? After which, I shall, of course, avail myself of your unparalleled generosity. Or do I perhaps need your consent in writing first? No? Then—*avanti*!'

* * *

In spite of some formidable past competition, it was quite the most difficult meal she had ever eaten in his company.

Except that she didn't really eat it, but merely pushed the food round her plate as if doing so.

Angelo, however, much to her resentment, ate everything placed in front of him as though he did not have a care in the world, or a thought in his head besides the enjoyment of his cook's delicious food.

Afterwards, in the *salotto*, he swallowed his coffee as if his throat was lined with asbestos, then offered her a smile which did not reach his eyes.

'I think it is time to retire, *carissima*. I shall inform your maid that her services will not be required tonight. I look forward to joining you *prima possibile*.'

'As soon as possible.' The loaded words tormented her all the way upstairs to her room.

She undressed and washed, before slipping into one of the chiffon and lace nightgowns provided in her trousseau. Then, sitting at her dressing table, she began to brush her hair, just as she had done on her wedding night, seeking once again a tranquillity which was beyond her.

Maybe, she thought, swallowing, she should simply settle for courage instead. Or at least the ability to conceal she was trembling inside.

She had just put the brush down and got to her feet when Angelo came noiselessly into the room, wearing his usual black silk robe. He paused, looking her up and down, his mouth twisting.

'Is it not a little late for such modesty?' he asked ironically. 'Particularly when your virginity is about to be sacrificed.'

Colour burned in her face. 'Please,' she said in a low voice. 'Please don't say things like that.'

'Ah,' he said. 'I see. You may treat me as if I were the dirt on your shoe, but I must still behave with consideration. Is that it?'

Ellie stood where she was, looking wretchedly down at the floor, and heard him sigh, quickly and sharply.

He said, 'It is still not too late, Elena. We can forget every-thing that has been said today—put the last months behind us, if you will come to me now as my bride on our marriage night.' His voice was low and very gentle. 'Trust me, *mia cara*, with your innocence and, this first time, give yourself to me completely so that we can remember it with joy for the rest of our lives.'

Ellie walked to the bed, and slid under the covers, remem-bering with a stab of pain how Silvia's hand had touched them in possession. Had in the past touched *him*...

She kept her tone cool. 'I think you have enough memories, *signore*. I have no wish to add to your tally.'

For a moment, he was very still. When he spoke, his voice was harsh. 'I shall not ask again. Let it be as you wish.'

He flung off the robe and got into bed beside her, propping himself on an elbow as he looked down at her. He muttered what was undoubtedly an obscenity under his breath, then drew her towards him, under him, his hand stroking the skirts of her nightdress away from her body as he did so, before parting her thighs.

Eyes closed, Ellie experienced the first intimate touch of a man's fingers. She had quite deliberately made him angry, yet this initial exploration was gentler than she'd expected—or probably deserved—and she felt sudden shame mingled with another emotion, less easy to decipher.

Angelo sighed again, very quietly this time, and his other hand lifted to cup one small pointed breast through its veil of chiffon, his thumb moving softly, rhythmically against the nipple until Ellie pushed it fiercely away.

'Don't!'

'*Carissima*,' he whispered urgently. 'I am not some brute. Must I be denied one caress—or even a kiss?'

Yes, she thought, you must. Because I want to be able to protect myself by hating you, so that I'll never be tempted to allow you near me in any way or to want more than this.

But she said nothing and, after a brief hesitation, he reached for one of the pillows, and slid it under her hips, raising her towards him. He lifted himself above her, and she felt the velvet hardness of him in stark and powerful arousal between her thighs, and a shiver of apprehension ran through her at what she had invited.

She thought wildly—This can't happen. It's not possible. Then Angelo moved unhurriedly and with great precision, taking himself *there* to the hidden centre of her womanhood and beginning slowly and carefully to enter her, resting his weight on his clenched fists on either side of her body.

She heard his terse whisper warning her to relax.

Yet there was no pain. What disturbed her most was the total strangeness of the sensation—and the way her untried, unbidden flesh seemed so ready, even eager to yield in order to accommodate him and further his total possession of her.

She had not, she thought dazedly, bargained for that particular danger.

Although her eyes were still shut tight, some instinct told her that he was looking down at her, the dark gaze searching her face for signs of discomfort or fear, and she had to fight an almost overwhelming impulse to reassure him in some way. To touch his face, or his hair, maybe even to slide her arms round his neck.

Which, of course, was sheer madness, but, then, nothing that was happening seemed to be real. Except, she thought, for his body, which with one last measured thrust, was now completely sheathed inside hers. His voice saying quietly, 'Is it well with you, Elena? I need you to tell me.'

And her whispered, 'Yes.'

In spite of everything, he was trying to be kind, she thought, bewildered, even as some female instinct she'd not known she possessed told her that, if she had let him, he could have been so much more than that.

He began to move inside her, gently at first, then more forcefully, withdrawing a little, then pushing back ever more deeply, awakening new and threatening feelings. Making her realise with alarm she would have to fight her body's wish to respond to the imperative drive of his loins as their force increased.

That there was an unfamiliar tide rising in her bloodstream, her bones, her skin, nudging at every atom of her consciousness that threatened to overwhelm her, urging her to lift her hips in answer to each warm and silken thrust. To make demands that were all her own.

And then—it was over. She heard his breathing change, quicken. He threw back his head, his voice crying out harshly almost bitterly and she felt a spurt of scalding heat far within her. Then he was still and there was silence.

For a moment or two, Angelo remained where he was, head bent, chest heaving, sweat slicking the bronzed shoulders, then, with the same care he'd shown her when it began, he lifted himself away from her, lying supine at her side, one arm resting across his closed eyes.

Ellie lay still too, her heartbeat going crazy as she attempted to adjust to what had happened. The words, 'It could have been so much worse,' were running through her brain like a ribbon unwinding, but she was not sure she believed them. Instead, and with even greater difficulty, she had to face what might have been...

He had done exactly what she'd told him she would accept, she thought. No more, no less. She had faced him and won, so why did she suddenly feel as if she had lost? Because that made no sense—no sense at all.

She turned her head slowly to look at him just as Angelo sat up abruptly, swinging his legs to the floor, and reaching down for his discarded robe.

'Congratulations, Elena.' He tossed the words over his shoulder. 'You have survived your ordeal with great fortitude. Let us hope for both our sakes that you will soon have good news for me, so that you are never called upon to endure it again.'

She watched him walk to the door. Her lips parted to say something—she wasn't sure what, it might have been just his name—then the door closed behind him, and she realised it was too late.

Too late, she repeated silently, and turned over, burying her face in the pillow.

The following April

She had learned long ago how to conduct herself at all these social events which Angelo required her to attend at his side.

Had mastered how to walk in with her hand resting lightly on his arm, and her smile already nailed securely in place. To offer all the appearance of a cherished young wife blissfully approaching the first anniversary of her wedding to one of the most glamorous men in the city. And to dazzle them with the diamonds and other jewels that would be regarded as an overt sign of Count Manzini's satisfaction with his marriage.

Knowing that none of the eyes watching them—friendly, inimical, admiring or jealous—must be allowed to catch even a glimpse of the reality of her abject failure and his bitter disappointment. Their mutual ongoing nightmare.

Tonight—a charity reception which Contessa Cosima was helping to host in aid of an orphanage—was an occasion like any other. She moved slowly round the room, slender in her black dress, the drink in her hand virtually untouched, pausing to greet acquaintances, to laugh and talk for a while before moving on, her timing immaculate, her appearance serene.

But underneath it all, her stomach was churning as she contemplated the end of the evening, the return to Vostranto and, later still, the promise of her husband's brief, monthly visit to her bedroom, conducted as always with cool efficiency and dispatch. Her terms strictly adhered to in every respect. The only verbal exchange between them Angelo's polite enquiry about her physical comfort as he took her.

Also just an occasion like any other, she told herself, her throat tightening. That was how she had to look at it, anyway, even when it could mean going to him eventually to tell him she had not conceived this time either. Just as she'd done every month up to now.

But maybe it wouldn't be like that, she thought. Maybe tonight, Nature would relent and her magic trick would work, as it had done only a few weeks ago for Tullia.

And if Ellie's delighted congratulations to her friend had

concealed different emotional strata, she was the only one who'd known it.

'And you, too, must have a baby very soon, Elena,' Tullia had declared buoyantly, hugging her. 'Then the children can play together.'

Zia Dorotea had sniffed and looked on the verge of launching some tart remark, but subsided after meeting Nonna Cosima's steady look.

Tonight, Angelo's grandmother was seated in a high-backed chair at the side of the room, and she smiled and beckoned when she saw Ellie.

'*Mia cara*, I wish you to meet my dear friend, Mother Felicitas. She is the superior of the Daughters of the Nativity who run the orphanage for us.'

The woman beside her was small and rosy-cheeked with sparkling dark eyes, wearing an ankle-length grey dress and a crisply starched white headdress and veil.

'This is a great pleasure, Contessa.' An appraising glance accompanied her handshake. 'We have always been blessed by the support of the Manzini family, and your godmother, the Principessa Damiano is another benefactor.'

She smiled. 'I am told that, unlike the Count's late mother and grandmother, you are a working wife, but I hope that in the future we can also persuade you to find time in your busy life for us. It would be an honour.'

Ellie coloured faintly. 'I—I'd really like that. Although I've never had a great deal to do with children.'

'But all that will change for you soon, I expect.' Mother Felicitas's glance was kind as she rose to her feet. 'That is life's way.'

'Yes,' Ellie agreed quietly. 'I—I hope so.'

'I must go now,' the nun added. 'Good night, my dear Cosima, and thank you for all you do for our children. Please bring Count Angelo's charming wife to visit us soon. We would be so delighted.'

'Come and sit with me, my child,' Nonna Cosima said when

Mother Felicitas had gone. 'You look a little pale this evening. You are not working too hard?'

'I don't think so.'

'Angelo is spending longer hours at Galantana than anyone can remember,' his grandmother continued musingly. 'And still using his apartment in the city while he does so, it seems.' She paused. 'I hope you are making time for each other in all this ceaseless industry. That is what a marriage needs, dearest girl, in order to succeed.'

Ellie bent her head. 'It also requires a couple who love each other,' she said in a low voice. 'And who weren't forced together for the sake of some outmoded convention.'

'Is that how it still seems to you?' Cosima Manzini queried softly. 'I am sorry to hear it.' She gave a faint rueful smile. 'I would not deny that my grandson has serious flaws, but I had hoped that, by now, he might have found a way of recommending himself to you as a husband, Elena. That you would be building a life together.'

Whereas, thought Ellie with a pang, we've never been further apart. And the fact that Angelo spends so much time in Rome should be a relief, but in another way it's sheer torture.

Because I know the way we live at Vostranto—the fact that there's no real intimacy in our lives and that the time we've spent in bed together since we were married can probably be measured in hours—and I realise that can't possibly be enough for him.

Because he's a man who has needs that I wouldn't know how to fulfil, even if I wanted to, and when I'm with him at a function like this, or at a dinner party and I see how the women look at him, I find, in spite of myself, that I'm wondering where he really spends his nights in Rome—and with whom.

Whether any of the girls who smile and chatter to me are really laughing at me behind my back—the dull wife, not only betrayed but apparently barren too.

And I'll wonder tonight, as I always do when he comes to me, if he's secretly glad not to have to pretend a desire he doesn't feel. Then I'll close my eyes and dig my nails in the palms of my hands and keep very still trying not to think of anything at all—or feel anything at all which is getting more and more difficult each time. And when he goes back to his own room and I'm alone, I'll lie awake for hours, trying not to cry, or—even worse—to follow him and ask—beg...

She looked down at her hands, clasped tightly in her lap. 'I don't think that's really feasible. We just aren't—suited to each other.'

'I am grieved to hear you say it.' Nonna Cosima's voice was very quiet. 'You see, *mia cara*, we thought long before that night at Largossa—your godmother and I—Dorotea too—that you would make Angelo an ideal wife. That you would find your match in each other.' She sighed. 'It seems we were not as clever as we thought.'

Ellie was silent for a moment, then she said, stumbling a little, 'Did Angelo also know what you thought—what you wanted?'

The older woman hesitated 'Dear child, it was no secret that his family—his friends felt it was high time he was married.'

'But I—I'd been—suggested?'

'Mentioned, perhaps, no more.'

'I see.' Ellie rose, smoothing her dress. 'It—explains a great deal.' *And makes me understand why there was really no escape—for either of us...*

'Elena.' Nonna Cosima took her hand, her eyes anxious. 'Promise me that Angelo is not unkind to you.'

'No,' Ellie returned after a pause. 'Under the circumstances, he's very—considerate. And generous too.' She touched fleetingly the diamonds in her ears and at her throat, forcing a smile. 'I really have nothing to complain about.'

She bent and kissed the scented cheek, smiled again in what she hoped was reassurance, then walked away.

Her circuit of the room completed, and her duty done, she looked round for Angelo and saw him several yards away, head slightly bent while he listened with rapt and smiling attention to what was being said to him. As she started towards him, the groups of people around him moved slightly, giving her a clearer view and she realised that his companion was Silvia, standing so near him that their bodies were almost touching as she looked up into his eyes, lips pouting, and one crimson tipped hand resting on his sleeve as if to emphasise the closeness of their association.

Ellie halted, shocked and turned away abruptly, nearly cannoning into a waiter carrying drinks. She muttered an apology then tossed the remaining wine in her glass down her throat before grabbing another from the tray, and swallowing a third of its contents in one gulp before heading for one of the long windows that had been opened on to the balcony beyond.

It had rained earlier, and there was a freshness in the air to combat the traffic fumes from the streets below. Ellie leaned on the wrought iron rail, aware of a trembling sensation in the pit of her stomach.

Her husband, she thought, with Silvia—as if time had somehow rolled back and they had regained their former intimacy. But how could it have happened?

Since her unexpected descent on Vostranto the previous year, and the quarrel that it had provoked, her cousin's name had not been mentioned. Nor had she been encountered at any of the social events that Ellie had attended, largely, she'd supposed, because Silvia would not find the company sufficiently entertaining.

Yet here she was at the kind of function she would normally have avoided. Unless, of course, she had good reason to be there...

Ellie took another mammoth swallow of wine, feeling the jolt of it curl down to her toes, although it didn't totally dispel that strange inner shaking as she'd hoped.

It was one thing to tell herself that Angelo would not feel obliged to remain faithful, and quite another to face the reality of his betrayal of his marriage vows—and with Silvia.

Did her cousin simply have to crook her little finger and watch him come running? she asked herself, anger building inside her. Was Angelo's desire for her so overwhelming that he could now overlook everything else that had happened—the selfish, vengeful trick she had played on both of them?

'Well,' she said aloud. 'If so, I don't have to wait around and watch.'

She finished the last of her wine, left the glass on a convenient ledge, and, feeling oddly empowered, walked back into the room and headed for the door.

A hand fell on her arm, halting her. 'Where have you been?' Angelo demanded. 'I have been looking for you.'

'I've been playing the part of your wife,' she said. 'And now I'm going to have the car brought round and go home.'

'Without a word to me?' His brows lifted. 'How was I supposed to get back to Vostranto?'

'I intended to leave a message. And I imagined you would spend the night in Rome,' she said. 'As you so often do.'

He said silkily, 'Not when I have one of my rare appointments with you, *mia bella*. An occasion not to be missed, believe me.'

'Indeed? Then I'm afraid, for once, you'll have to excuse me.'

His mouth curled. 'You are developing a headache, perhaps? The usual reason for a wife to evade her husband's attentions.'

'No,' she said, forcing her voice to speak coolly, dispassionately. 'Nothing like that. I've simply decided I just can't do this any more. And therefore I'd prefer to be alone tonight.'

'And if I wish to adhere to my own preferences?'

There was a note in his voice she'd never heard before, but her eyes were steady as they met the anger in his. Her tone was level too. 'Then your *signoria* will have to use force. Or accept that we're better apart.'

'Yes,' he said. 'Perhaps that would be safer—for tonight at least. So, I shall not detain you further.' He stepped back, making her a slight formal bow. *'Arrivederci, carissima.'*

'Goodnight,' Ellie whispered, and went to the door, fighting an impulse to look back and see if he was watching her leave.

Or whether he had already turned away in search of Silvia.

Because that was something she found she could not bear to know.

CHAPTER NINE

SHE AWOKE SLOWLY, and lay for a moment totally disorientated, staring at plain white walls and spring sunlight lying slatted across the polished boards of the floor, wondering why the bed was so much narrower, and why Donata was not here opening the shutters and bringing her morning coffee.

Of course, she thought. I must have been having a dream about Vostranto. That's what threw me. But I'm actually at Casa Bianca. I drove down to Porto Vecchio yesterday. And I'm not going back.

A week had passed since the night of the reception. Seven days and nights had come and gone without a word from Angelo. He was in Rome, and she was at his house in the hills, but the real distance between them covered continents rather than miles.

'Better apart' she had told him, and it seemed that he now agreed with her, she'd told herself as she roamed restlessly round Vostranto. That he accepted that they should put an end to this ill-assorted marriage and start their lives again.

After all, she reasoned, there was nothing to keep them together, not even the hope of a baby, and she would agree without argument to whatever means he chose to achieve their mutual freedom.

She had her work—almost more than she could handle if she was honest—and she would find another apartment somewhere in the city. Re-start her life as it had been, and find some peace. Regard the last months as a mistake—serious but not irretrievable.

She'd tried very hard during his absence not to think about him. Not to wonder where he was and what he did once the working day was over. Above all, she worked on not speculating who he might be with, especially now that she had the image etched on her mind of Silvia's hand curling possessively round his sleeve to go with that other memory of her standing smiling at the bed she planned to share with him, as she'd done from the first.

Angelo must have decided that, in spite of everything she'd done, her cousin was the woman he really wanted. That she was too deep in his bloodstream for him to turn away again, and he would forgive her as everyone had always forgiven Silvia, because beauty was its own excuse.

He must genuinely love her, Ellie thought. And, in the end, that was all that mattered. Wasn't it? She had to believe it was true, anyway.

And she—she would be Ellie Blake again, instead of this strange manufactured creature masquerading as the Contessa Manzini. She'd always felt that she was filling someone else's shoes, and, no matter how she'd been dressed up, she'd never looked the part as Silvia, beautiful, stylish and totally single-minded, undoubtedly would.

She could only hope that her cousin would love Vostranto as much as she'd done and be content there, rather than regarding it as just another glamorous Manzini asset and hankering for the hectic social life of the city.

But that, she thought, would not be her problem. And perhaps, because she'd won as she always insisted on doing, Silvia's attitude would change.

Whatever, there was nothing now to hold Angelo back from pursuing her again. He'd got his investment and the Galantana expansion was forging ahead, so the prospect of scandal over her divorce from Ernesto would no longer be of any great concern.

And Ellie resolved that she would play her part—assuring

her godmother and Prince Damiano that her marriage to Angelo would never have worked in a thousand years. Making it clear that it was no-one's fault, that as a couple they would always be chalk and cheese, oil and water, so that bringing the whole unfortunate fiasco to an end had to be the best solution for all involved.

That she herself found the decision an actual relief.

All the same, there would be anger, she knew and disappointment. She could imagine Nonna Cosima's sadness, and Madrina's bewilderment, while Zia Dorotea would have a field day, apportioning blame indiscriminately, and hoped they could understand why she had gone without saying goodbye to them.

Because she could never, ever explain why it had all become so impossible. Why she could no longer endure the dutiful ritual that might lead to conception from a man whose desires and passions had always been focussed elsewhere.

She could not even define to her own satisfaction why it had been so necessary for her to be the one to put an end to it all and walk away, and told herself it had to be pride.

Or perhaps it was the terse communication she'd eventually received from him by email, informing her that he would be returning at the weekend, because matters could not continue in this way between them and there were things that must be said.

She had sat staring at it, scanning the message over and over again, before pressing the delete button, because she knew these would be things she could not bear to hear.

Even if their marriage had been doomed from the outset, she'd played her part in its failure, she'd thought, as she went upstairs to begin preparations for her departure. And she could give no hint to anyone—Angelo least of all—that the prospect of Silvia's triumph was like the intolerable pain of a knife being turned in an open wound.

When she'd come down with her travel bag, smiling cheerfully, she'd told a concerned Assunta merely that she intended to have a little holiday, but her plans were fluid, and she was not sure when she would return. Which, she thought, was her only untruth.

And there had, of course, only ever been one place to come to.

She sat up slowly in the bed, pushing back her hair, looking round the familiar room. The cottage had always been her refuge, and never more so than now. It was her own space, she thought, with no disturbing resonances of anyone else.

As she pushed back the covers, she saw the faint pale mark on her finger where her wedding ring had been. She never wore it when she came down here, anyway, because it belonged to another life, which, for a short while she was leaving behind her.

But, this time she was going for good, so she'd left it in Angelo's bedroom with all the other jewellery he had given her, and her handwritten letter telling him simply that in view of the disaster their marriage had become, she was leaving in order to save them both further embarrassment and unhappiness. She added in conclusion that she wanted nothing from him except the legal dissolution of their relationship, and that she wished him well for the future.

She'd brought away little more than the clothes she stood up in. The designer gear on the padded silk hangers had never been her choice anyway, so she wouldn't miss it, and besides there was plenty of stuff here in the cupboard and drawers that suited her purpose far better—cotton skirts, pants and tops and some swimwear, although, admittedly, it was rather too early in the year for sea-bathing.

She padded barefoot out of the bedroom in her brief cotton nightshirt, and walked to the kitchen. Signora Alfredi, the stout elderly widow next door, who kept an eagle eye on Casa Bianca when Ellie was not there, had left a bag of groceries on the kitchen table, including some bread, sliced ham, eggs and a pack of coffee, so breakfast was taken care of.

Later, she would supplement her supplies at the local shops, and, for lunch, she would probably see what the fishing boats had brought in. Then, tonight, she would eat as usual in the little *trattoria* on the quayside, where Santino and Maria would welcome her back.

My routine, she thought, spooning coffee into the machine. Sweet and reassuringly familiar. As if I'd never been away and the last wretched months had never happened. This is what I need. And it's all I need.

Yet in spite of her resolution, it was a couple of days before Casa Bianca began to work its usual magic. She slept poorly for one thing, and was glad she could not remember her dreams. Also she found it difficult to concentrate on her work, making elementary and annoying mistakes.

After one particularly trying session, she decided to close down her laptop and get some fresh air to see if that would get rid of the cobwebs in her mind.

On the way out, she called at Signora Alfredi's house to pick up her dog, Poco, who was her usual companion on such walks. He was an odd-looking little animal, with a round amiable face, drooping ears, a long body and short legs, and he possessed seemingly boundless energy. However, the Signora's health and increasing girth meant she could not give him the exercise he needed, so this had become a task which Ellie gladly assumed when she stayed at the cottage.

He scampered happily beside her along the promenade and down the shallow flight of wooden steps to the almost deserted beach, then took off like a rocket along the sand with a bark of sheer joy, eventually returning with a piece of stick that Ellie was required to throw for him. A game, experience told her, that she would tire of long before he did.

In spite of a breeze from the sea, there was real heat in the sun today, and she moved her shoulders pleasurably inside her thin shirt as she walked along the edge of the water, watching the golden light dance on its ripples.

When Poco returned from his umpteenth foray, once more dropping his stick expectantly at her feet, she picked it up and, slipping off her espadrilles, ran laughing into the shallows, splashing along regardless of the soaking of her white cut-offs as the dog chased her, yapping excitedly, leaping up to retrieve his treasure which she was holding teasingly just out of reach.

Suddenly she felt exhilarated, the sense of freedom she'd longed for actually within reach as she danced in and out of the water, singing to herself.

When eventually, she turned to run back the way she'd come, something made her glance up at the promenade, and, in the blinding dazzle of the sun, she seemed to catch a glimpse of a man's dark figure standing there motionless, as if watching her. Blinking, she put up a hand to shield her eyes, but when she looked again there was no-one there.

I can't sleep, she thought in self-derision, and now I'm seeing things. Time to get a grip, Ellie my dear.

She threw the stick for Poco one last time, then called him to heel and went home.

The *trattoria* was busy that evening, enjoying its usual brisk local trade. Ellie made her way to her corner table, acknowledging the smiling greetings from other diners, and sat down, in the comfortable certainty that Santino would soon appear with her Campari and soda.

The plate of mixed meats that would precede her asparagus risotto had just been placed in front of her when she became aware that the hum of conversation around her had suddenly stilled—that something like a *frisson* had run through the crowded room.

She looked up and saw the reason, her eyes widening involuntarily.

He was standing in the doorway, glancing round him, relaxed and faintly smiling as he took in his surroundings. Assured and undeniably good-looking, she summarised him objectively, as if completing some mental check list. Casually but expensively dressed. And sexy in a way that transcended mere looks. Even across a crowded room.

Someone she'd never seen at Santino's before—or anywhere else in Porto Vecchio for that matter, otherwise she'd have remembered, along with every other woman in the room.

But however memorable, he was simply not her type, she told herself, dismissively. Experience, it seemed, had the distinct advantage of conferring immunity.

Although, to give him his due, the newcomer seemed oblivious to the effect he was having on the female clientele at large.

Ellie decided that he must be staying at the big white hotel on the promontory, which was pricey and fairly formal and had just re-opened for the summer. Quite a few of its residents, especially the foreign tourists, eventually found their way down to the port in search of less stuffy surroundings. But not usually so early in their stay, she thought drily, then realised with shock that he was strolling towards her corner.

Oh, no, she thought with sudden breathlessness. This couldn't be happening. It wasn't possible…

'*Buona sera, signorina.*' The swift charm of his smile touched her like a finger stroking her cheek as she looked up, stiffening defensively. 'As we are both unaccompanied tonight, I hope you will allow me to join you.'

'No! I mean—I don't think so.' She set down her glass with something of a jerk. 'I'd prefer to be alone, thank you.'

His shrug was graceful. '*Che peccato.* I am desolated.' He paused. 'Do you think you might relent by the time coffee is served?'

She swallowed. 'I'm afraid I won't be staying that long, but—but have a pleasant meal,' she added almost wildly.

'I am sure I will,' he returned. 'But it could have been a delight.'

Very smooth, Ellie thought stonily, as he walked away and she addressed herself to the Parma ham on her plate. But cuts no ice with me.

All the same, she'd found the incident disturbing, even though she felt she'd handled it well, letting him see that any approach was unacceptable. But it was annoying that the only free table was right in her sightline against the opposite wall, so that she only had to look up to see him there. And to find that, most of the time, he was looking right back at her, his gaze intent, even considering.

He has no right to do that, she thought smouldering. No right at all. Why couldn't he have stayed where he belonged—up at the hotel or—wherever?

However, she was careful to complete her meal without undue haste, choosing *panna cotta* served with a fruit *coulis* for dessert, then paid her bill and left, staring rigidly ahead to ensure there was not one more atom of eye contact. Safely outside, she was almost tempted to run, but told herself she was being ridiculous.

For one thing, the newcomer was far too occupied with Santino's *pollo Milanese*, while, for another, and more importantly, he had almost certainly got the message by now. For his kind, making a beeline for any single woman in his orbit was a mere reflex action like breathing, and she'd be stupid to read any more into it than that.

It was just that it had been—so unexpected. Nothing like it had ever happened to her before. And she could not risk getting involved.

The wisest course would be to pretend it had never happened at all. Anyway, if he began to be a real nuisance, she would only have to tell Santino, and he would be instantly warned off. Porto Vecchio, after all, was full of people who remembered Nonna Vittoria with deep affection.

But it would not come to that. He was probably not used to rejection, especially in public, she thought as she let herself into the house, but it would do him a world of good. So, tomorrow night, with luck, he would eat back at his hotel, giving up as a bad job any random thoughts he might still be harbouring about her.

Although she hadn't the least idea why he should, she thought, examining herself critically in her bedroom mirror. She hadn't changed and suddenly become a beauty—an object of desire to an attractive man. And it wasn't as if she'd looked affluent wearing an old blue dress, much loved but faded by the sun, and with plain silver studs in her ears. So there'd been no reason for him to wish to spend even five minutes with her.

It makes no sense, she told herself. No sense at all. But it's over, so what does it matter?

She considered eating at home the following night, but told herself she'd be stupid to allow herself to be pressured out of her favourite restaurant on the off-chance some visiting glamour-boy might be present. And even if he did dine at Santino's, he would be unlikely to try again and risk a further snub.

And, in the event, he did not turn up, so she'd been worrying—if that was the word—about nothing. Though that had not prevented her looking up nervously each time anyone came into the *trattoria*.

Behaving like a cat on hot bricks, she derided herself, over someone who'd probably moved on by now to look for more excitement.

But she was mistaken as she discovered the following morning when she was on the beach with Poco and saw him walking towards them, long muscular legs and bronze arms displayed in shorts and a polo shirt.

'*Buongiorno*,' he greeted her pleasantly as he halted, looking up at the sky. 'They say it will rain later. Do you think so?'

'It's unlikely,' Ellie said shortly and would have walked on, except he'd crouched down, snapping his fingers and Poco, the treacherous mutt had gone straight to him and was lying across his sandaled foot, waving his paws in the air.

'Your dog at least seems to like me, *signorina*,' he commented as he gently rubbed the proffered tummy. 'What is his name?'

'He's my neighbour's dog,' Ellie said coldly. 'And his name is Poco.'

'An odd choice. He is hardly as small as all that.'

Ellie bit her lip. 'She told me she called him that because when he was a puppy, she asked his breed and they told her "A little of this and a little of that."'

'I think they told the truth.' He got lithely to his feet, tucking

Poco under his arm. 'My new friend and I are going to the *caffe* by the church. Would you care to come with us?'

'No, of course not!'

He said briskly, 'Then you had better tell me where you live so I can deliver Poco safely home when we have finished our refreshments.'

'But you can't do that,' Ellie said stormily.

'What is to prevent me? I wish it.' He gently pulled one of Poco's ears, and had his hand licked. 'And he is perfectly willing.'

'He's not your dog.'

'Nor yours, it seems. And I need my coffee,' he added. 'If you are so concerned for Poco's welfare, I suggest you join us.'

He set off across the sand to the promenade, and Ellie followed, angry to feel so helpless but knowing she had no choice, because there was no way she would allow him near Casa Bianca, whatever the excuse.

When they were seated at a table on the pavement, and she'd been served with a filter coffee while he chose espresso and a sweet roll which he shared with Poco who'd been brought a bowl of water, Ellie said tautly, 'Are you doing this to punish me?'

His brows lifted. 'For what?'

She met his gaze defiantly. 'For refusing to have dinner with you, of course.'

'Is the coffee here so bad it ranks as punishment?' He sounded faintly amused. 'I don't think so.'

'Then—why?'

'It is quite simple. The other morning, I saw a girl laughing and dancing in the sea as if she did not have one care in the world. I wanted to find out what could have prompted such happiness.'

So, she had not imagined that she was being watched. It was a disturbing thought and she made herself drink some coffee before she answered. 'I think—realising that I didn't have to be unhappy any longer.'

'What made you so sad?'

She looked away, her heart hammering. 'I don't want to discuss it.'

'Ah,' he said softly. 'Then it is a man.'

'No,' she denied swiftly. 'Or—not in the way you think.'

This is dangerous, she thought with a kind of desperation. I shouldn't be here. I shouldn't be doing this. I ought to leave the coffee, grab Poco—and go. Talking to him like this—being with him—is madness that I can't afford.

'How do you know what I think, *signorina*?'

'I don't,' she said. 'I don't know you, *signore*, or anything about you. And I'd prefer to keep it that way.' She rose. 'Now, Signora Alfredi will be wondering where we are, so if you'll excuse me...'

'On one condition,' he said. As she passed his chair to retrieve the dog, he put a hand on her arm. 'That you have dinner with me tonight.'

'That's quite impossible.' She looked down at the darkness of the tanned fingers against the comparative pallor of her own skin, her throat tightening uncontrollably. 'And don't touch me—please.'

His hand lifted immediately, unquestioningly. 'But we both have to eat,' he said. 'Shall we meet at the *trattoria* at nine, or should I collect you from your house?'

'No!' The word sounded almost anguished, and she paused, taking a deep breath. Be careful, she thought. Be very careful. 'Anyway, you don't know where I live.'

'It would not be hard to discover.' He smiled faintly. 'Maria at the restaurant has a romantic heart, I think.'

Romantic... The word seemed to judder in her mind.

She said, her voice taut, 'Please understand, *signore*, that there is no possibility of—romance between us, and there never will be.'

He leaned back, the dark eyes speculative. 'But, *signorina*, how can you be so sure?'

She scooped up a wriggling Poco. 'Because I am married,' she said stonily. 'And one bitter experience is quite enough in anyone's lifetime. Does that answer your question? Now please leave me alone.'

And she walked away, without looking back.

She was restless all day, unable to settle to the translation work awaiting her attention, or, if she was honest, to very much at all. And she didn't need this kind of distraction, she told herself angrily. She'd come here for peace and quiet. To find herself again. Perhaps even—to heal…

Not to engage in a reluctant battle of wits with someone she didn't know—and didn't want to know.

She was tempted to pack her bag, lock up Casa Bianca, walk up to the square where her car was parked—and go.

But where? Not back to Vostranto, that was for sure. And turning up at the Palazzo Damiano would involve a lot of questions she would prefer not to answer—or not immediately.

Besides, why should she be the one to leave? She belonged here and he most certainly didn't. So, he had no right to intrude like this and turn her small private world upside down. Amusing himself at her expense by this—totally meaningless pursuit.

A man, she thought, fuelling her resentment, who'd never learned to be kind, because he hadn't found it necessary. Who was accustomed, instead, to using his surface attraction in order to gain easy favour. And wasn't used to taking 'no' for an answer.

Only, it wasn't going to work. Not with her. So he could just—pack his designer luggage and move on. Go back to playing his games with people who knew the rules.

But until he did so, she was damned if he was going to turn her into a prisoner in her own home. Or a fugitive.

Yes, she would eat at the *trattoria* tonight, she decided, squaring her slender shoulders, because that was how she lived when she was here, and his presence would not deter her, or the probability that he would manoeuvre her somehow into sharing his table.

And if that prospect, and the memory of their previous

encounters, was preventing her concentration on the job in hand, she would find something else to occupy her.

With a suggestion of gritted teeth, she embarked on a heavy-duty clean of the living room, moving furniture, scrubbing the floor and even washing walls, before moving on to the kitchen, the shower room and finally her bedroom. The two empty rooms at the rear of the cottage which in Nonna Vittoria's day had provided the accommodation for family holidays she decided to leave for another day.

When evening came, she showered and washed her hair, drying it to hang casually loose and shining round her face, then dressed in slim white cotton pants, and a dark red top even more elderly than the blue dress. She reached for her scent spray only to put it back, unused, together with her cosmetic bag.

This rendezvous was not of her choosing, she reminded herself, viewing herself with indifference, so there was no compulsion to make an effort. Exactly the opposite, in fact.

She walked slowly to the restaurant, her hands clenched into fists in her pockets as she strove for an appearance of composure.

He was there, as she'd known he would be, seated at a table set for two with flowers, candles lit, and chilled white wine, while Maria, of the romantic soul, waited, eyes dancing to usher her there.

He got to his feet, relaxed in chinos and a white shirt, its cuffs rolled back over his forearms, his smile glinting.

He said softly, 'So you came. I was not sure that you would.'

'Really?' She took her seat. 'Now I'd have said you'd never suffered a moment's uncertainty in your entire life, *signore*.'

'Then perhaps you should not judge by appearances, *signorina*.' He paused. 'But must we be so formal?' He offered her a swift smile. 'My name is Luca. And yours?'

Her hesitation was palpable. 'It's—Helen,' she said at last. The English version of her name, she thought, that only her parents had used. Something to hide behind.

He inclined his head. '*Buonasera*, Helen. It is good to meet you.'

She looked down at the white cloth. 'It's hardly the first time.'

'Then let us make it so.' He signalled to Santino, who came to pour the cold, sparkling wine into the waiting flutes. He added softly, 'To your good health,' as he raised his glass.

The wine tingled against the dryness of her mouth and throat. She said huskily, 'I don't know what I'm doing here. This is such a mistake.'

'Why do you say that?'

She stared at the bubbles in her glass. 'You—you already know.'

'Ah,' Luca said. 'Because you are married.' He reached out and took her hand, his thumb smoothing the pale band of skin where her wedding ring had been. 'But it is not an easy thing to remember.'

His touch was infinitely light, but it seemed to rip through her, making her heart pound unevenly, and she pulled her hand away, flushing. 'You've also forgotten that I—asked you not to touch me.'

'But that, I think, is impossible.'

She swallowed. Her voice was a thread. 'Then let me tell you this. Whatever you think is going to happen between us—you're wrong.'

'So, I shall have to live with disappointment,' he said lightly. 'However, we can still enjoy our food, I hope. I ordered for us in advance, *mia bella*—linguine with mussels and roasted sea bass. Do you approve?'

She bent her head. 'It sounds—delicious.'

'Good.' He raised his glass again, the dark gaze intent, almost reflective in the candlelight. 'Then, *buon appetito*, Helen—for this—and whatever else tonight may bring. Even if it is—nothing.' And he drank to her.

CHAPTER TEN

'So,' LUCA SAID, sampling the *zabaglione* which he'd chosen for their dessert. 'Tell me about your husband.'

Ellie put down her spoon, startled. His behaviour over the meal had been impeccable, keeping the conversation general, light and amusing, encouraging her to relax and enjoy each excellent course, even to smile and respond shyly to his practised banter. Yet now he'd suddenly switched to the personal again. The much too personal. And she wasn't sure how to handle it.

She took a breath. 'There's nothing to tell,' she countered.

'Nothing?' he queried lightly. 'So, does he even exist, I wonder, or is he an invention to keep unwanted lovers at bay?'

She made herself eat some of the frothy concoction in front of her. 'He's real enough,' she said eventually. 'But I can't describe him, because I don't know him, or anything about him and I never have.'

His brows lifted. 'You married a complete stranger?'

'It was an arrangement,' she said. 'Forced on us both by circumstance.'

'I believe such arrangements can sometimes turn out well,' he said, after a silence. 'With a little goodwill on both sides.'

'Perhaps.' Ellie couldn't eat any more and put down her spoon. 'But—not in this case.'

'You seem very sure.'

'I've had plenty of time to decide.' *And now, because of*

Silvia, I have a convincing reason too... 'And concluded that I should leave.'

'And came here.' His tone was reflective. 'Will you tell me why?'

'Because I knew it was the last place that he—my husband—would ever come to.'

Luca frowned. 'What is wrong with it?'

Ellie shrugged. 'Oh—it's not vibrant—or glamorous—or full of the beautiful people—like those he went ski-ing with last winter,' she added.

'But you did not accompany him.' A statement rather than a question.

She shook her head. 'I don't ski.'

'You could learn. Or you could simply enjoy the air and the beauty of the mountains as many do without venturing on to the slopes.'

That, she thought, was what Tullia had said. 'Oh, do come with us, Elena,' she'd appealed. 'We can find a nice terrace and sit with our hot chocolate and wonderful cakes while Angelo and Domenico and the others go off on their black runs.

'Besides, Mamma was saying the other day that you and Angelo have still not had a honeymoon.' She'd looked at Ellie with dancing eyes. 'Perhaps in such a romantic place, he will wish to treat this as one.'

And she'd replied, forcing herself to smile back, her heart pounding, even though the prospect of sharing a room and a bed with him for the duration had been one of the main deterrents, 'A little too public, don't you think? Anyway I'd probably do something silly—slip on the ice and break something and spoil his plans. Believe me, I'm far better off staying at Vostranto.'

Tullia had pouted, but when she returned, she had little to say about the trip other than Ellie was probably right not to have gone, and would have been bored.

Angelo had said even less.

Now, striving for lightness, and a way to bring the conversation and the evening to a speedy end, she said, 'Maybe I'm just the indoor type.'

'And yet you spend part of each day on the beach.'

'That's quite different. When I'm here, I'm alone—and free.'

He looked at her unsmilingly. 'Is that what I saw that first morning—a dance of freedom?'

'I—I don't know.' Had it been freedom, she wondered, that inexplicable, overwhelming sense of irresistible joy that had so unexpectedly assailed her, as if some locked door had suddenly opened on to a new and hopeful world? And all she had to do was hold out her hand to claim it for her own?

Before, of course, she realised what was awaiting her...

Hurriedly, she pushed back her chair and reached for her bag. 'Anyway, I must be going,' she said.

'You do not wish for coffee and some strega, perhaps, or sambucca?'

'*No, grazie.* But it was a wonderful meal,' she added politely. 'So, if you will excuse me, *signore.*'

He rose too. 'May it not be Luca?'

She swallowed. 'If that is—really what you want.'

'Indeed it is,' he said. '*Buona notte*, Helen. I wish you pleasant dreams.' He paused. 'And I look forward to meeting you on the beach tomorrow.'

'I—I may not be there. I have—things to do.'

'Then Poco and I will both be disappointed.' He walked round the table, took her hand and raised it to his lips. 'And as I am now convinced you are married,' he said softly, 'what can you possibly have to fear?'

And that, thought Ellie as she gave him a taut smile before heading for the door, was the six-million-dollar question.

She lay for a long time that night staring into the darkness, her mind endlessly reviewing every word that had been spoken between them, her inner vision possessed by images of him in almost frightening detail—the turn of his head, the length of the black eyelashes, the shape of his mouth. As if, she thought, she'd been gazing at him all evening, committing him to some private corner of her memory, instead of trying to avoid glancing at him at all.

Under her nightshirt, her body was tingling, her nipples hard against the thin fabric, scalding heat between her thighs.

Oh God, this is so wrong, she told herself, turning over to bury her flushed face in the pillow. Wrong and crazy. I don't recognise myself any more, or know what I'm doing, and that scares me. Because there are so many reasons why I shouldn't be thinking about him—ever, and the fact that I'm still technically a married woman is probably the least of them.

'Luca,' she whispered under her breath. 'Luca—why did I have to meet you now? Why couldn't it have been long ago when everything was different? When I was different?'

She fell asleep at last, but woke again at sunrise. She showered, put on her robe, then worked doggedly for several hours, drinking cups of black coffee and not allowing herself to think of anything else while she caught up with her schedule.

This was her real life, she thought, as she finally closed down her laptop, and she must never forget that. Must take care to ignore any temptation to wonder if it could ever have been otherwise.

She did some washing and hung it in the small courtyard at the back of the house. It was going to be the warmest day yet, she realised, looking up at the sun, high in an almost cloudless sky. A foretaste of summer heat, and there was little breeze so the sea would be like a millpond.

She fought with herself as she tidied an already tidy house, repeating over and over again that she would be a fool and worse than a fool to go anywhere near the beach today whatever the weather. But, as she'd known from the first, it was a losing battle, so she changed into a bikini, covered it with shorts and a cheesecloth shirt, put sun lotion, a towel, some bottled water and an apple in a canvas bag and headed for the shore.

She had just reached the steps when Luca's hand descended lightly on her shoulder. *'Buon giorno,'* he said. 'Where is your little friend today?'

She said stiltedly, 'The Signora's niece is taking her out for the day, and Poco is going too. The children adore him.'

'Ah.' His brows lifted. 'So, is it possible for you to tolerate my company alone?'

He was wearing khaki shorts, and espadrilles, his sun glasses pushed up on top of his head, and the rest of him was bare bronze skin. The faint amusement in his dark eyes was also playing round his firm mouth, and every inch of him spelled danger.

She said huskily, 'I thought I might swim.'

'I thought so too. I was only waiting for you.'

'And if I'd stayed away?' *As I should have done...*

He shrugged a shoulder and she tried not to notice the play of muscle under the smooth skin. 'Then I would have come to find you.'

He had already spread a towel in the shelter of a rock, and she arranged hers beside it, fumbling a little as she felt tension building inside her.

He said gently, 'There is no need to be afraid.'

Now how did he know that? she wondered wildly. Aloud, she said, 'I—I don't understand what's happening. Why you are doing this, when you know—when I've told you the situation.'

'You have told me certain things.' The dark gaze held hers. 'But not all of it, I think.'

Ellie bit her lip. 'All that is possible, anyway.'

'At least until you begin to trust me,' he agreed, unzipping his shorts to reveal black swimming trunks.

Feeling absurdly self-conscious, Ellie discarded her own shorts and shirt, thankful that her dark green bikini was cut on lines more demure than strictly fashionable, but aware, just the same, of the frank appreciation in his expression.

Then he took her hand, and began to walk down the beach, his pace quickening until he was running with Ellie laughing and breathless at his side as they reached the water's edge, and splashed into the softly curling shallows.

For a moment the sea felt so cold it made her gasp, but Luca's arm was round her, urging her forward, making her forget her initial recoil as the water deepened.

And when the lean, brown body beside her dived forward into the waves, she followed, the chill suddenly becoming— exhilaration.

It had been months since her last swim, and all the bleak unhappiness and uncertainty she'd experienced during that time seemed to fall away from her, leaving her buoyant as the sunlit air as she cut through the water in her smooth, efficient crawl.

When she began to feel the pull on her muscles, she turned and swam back slowly to where Luca was waiting for her, treading water, his dark hair gleaming in the sun.

'You swim very well,' he said. 'Where did you learn?'

'Here,' she said. 'My father taught me when we came to stay with my grandmother.' She wrinkled her nose. 'I used to go to the public baths sometimes when I lived in Rome, although they were always so crowded. Several of my colleagues went to the big hotels to swim in their pools, but I found that too expensive.'

'*Che peccato,*' Luca said softly. 'Because I often did the same. We might have met much earlier.'

'I think I'd have been lost in the crowd.' *In so many ways...* She forced a smile. 'But that's why I'm out of practice and out of condition.'

'It is not apparent. You came here often as a child?'

'Whenever it was possible. We all loved it.' She paused. 'Nonna Vittoria's other daughter, my aunt and—and her family were never as keen.'

Now why, she wondered vexed, did I need to mention that?

She added hurriedly, 'And I love it still.'

'That is evident. But it is a pity that you come here alone.'

'I don't see it that way at all.' She began to swim back to the shore using a sedate breast-stroke. 'I'm quite happy in my own company.'

His voice reached her quietly. 'And that is an even greater

pity. A woman with such a gift for happiness should not prefer solitude.'

Once out of the water, Ellie walked quickly up the beach, aware of Luca keeping pace at her shoulder and the unruly hammering of her heart as she headed for the freshwater shower sited at the edge of the promenade to rinse the salt from her skin. She stepped into the shallow basin, and reached for the control lever only to find his hand covering hers as he joined her under the shower head, pulling her towards him.

She said in a voice she didn't recognise, 'No, please, you mustn't. It's not right...'

'Are you throwing your marriage in my face again, Helen?' His tone was harsh. 'The fact that you belong to another man? Do you wish he was here with you now instead of me—this husband?'

And this time her whispered 'No' was in acceptance, not denial, as Luca turned on the water and stood, holding her close against him so that she breathed the cool, salty fragrance of his skin as the cascade covered them both. She could feel the thud of his heart echoing through her own bloodstream, and leaned into him, resting her forehead against the muscularity of his chest, her legs shaking under her, waiting for what would be.

When the gush of water stopped, Luca put his hand under her chin, tilting her face up towards his. He said gently, 'I will say again—you have nothing to fear, I promise you. Nothing.' And let her go.

Afterwards, when they had gone back to the rock and dried themselves, Ellie produced her sun lotion and Luca lay, propped up on an elbow observing her, his dark gaze candidly intent, as she applied the liquid to her slender legs, her arms, her midriff, and, having carefully removed the halter strap, the faint swell of her breasts above the bikini top.

She said with a catch in her breath, 'Why are you watching me?'

'You know why, *mia bella.*' There was a smile in his voice, as he stretched out a hand for the bottle. 'So there is no need to play games. Permit me to attend to your back, *per favore.*'

She turned over, lying face downwards on her towel, her body rigid, hands clamped to her sides, trying to subdue the uncertain clamour of her pulses.

Luca began with her shoulders, his touch as gentle as she had hoped—or perhaps dreaded. As he smoothed the lotion into her heated skin with light, circular movements, Ellie found her fists slowly beginning to unclench and the tension in her muscles relaxing.

His hand moved downwards, and she flinched instinctively as he released the clip that fastened her bra.

'No—please.'

'Will it also please you to have a mark across your back?' he asked softly, as his fingertips anointed the delicate, untrammelled contour of her spine.

There seemed no answer to that, and the lingering stroke of his hands on her body was making her so breathless she probably couldn't have spoken anyway, she thought, closing her eyes and giving herself up to pure sensation.

He did not hurry, finishing his ministrations decorously about a centimetre above the band of her bikini briefs. 'Now you will not burn.'

But she was scorching already, every fibre of her being, each bone, each drop of blood in her starved body coming alive, its long-suppressed hunger crying out for appeasement—for a satisfaction that had up to now only existed in her imagination. That she had tried so hard to teach herself to live without, while struggling at the same time to endure those brief, unhappy encounters in the marriage bed. Until endurance threatened to turn into heartbreak and became utterly impossible.

A voice she did not recognise mumbled *'Grazie.'*

'Prego,' Luca returned and she felt the swift brush of his lips on the nape of her neck before he turned away to stretch out on his own towel.

She pretended to doze, keeping her eyes closed, letting her breathing slow to a quiet rhythm, but her body was wide-awake, in thrall to this delicious agony of need that his touch had engendered. Which he must realise, she thought unhappily. He was an experienced man who'd know exactly what effect even the most casual caress would have. Who intended it to arouse and incite. To make her want him.

Because—hadn't seduction been his purpose ever since he'd walked into the *trattoria* some forty eight hours earlier and seen her there? She swallowed. After all, he'd hardly made a secret of it. Had he? And her rejection of him had only made him more determined, if only to heal his damaged male ego.

I should never have let this begin, she thought desperately. I should have gone while I had the chance. Headed south. Found a small *pensione* somewhere equally unfashionable and played the waiting game until I could call Santino and check that Luca had gone and it was safe to return.

But it was pride that kept me here. Wanting to prove to myself that I could cope with the situation and keep him at arm's length. That very same pride that took me away from Vostranto. The need to convince myself that I was in charge of my own destiny and needed to take the initiative. To jump before I was pushed.

Yet how could I have imagined that something like this could ever happen? That he could suddenly appear like this, turning my life upside down, so that I no longer know what to do—or even who I am any more?

But it's left me with only one certainty—that if I let him any closer to me, I'll be lost forever, faced with a lifetime of regret. And I cannot afford that, especially when all he wants is a few hours' entertainment. Because there can't be any more to it than that and he has to know that. Has to…

And she went on lying silently there, only a few inches away from him, the ache of desire in her body fighting the turmoil in her mind. Knowing she would only have to stretch out a hand to touch him while reciting all the very real and cogent reasons to do no such thing.

Recalling another time when the urge to touch a man—to offer him her body—had almost overwhelmed her and reminding herself, too, of the unhappiness that would inevitably have followed if she'd given way. The shame she would have felt after revealing her innermost feelings and needs to someone whom she knew neither loved nor cared for her in the ways that mattered. The misery of discovering where his desires were truly centred.

Luca was the opposite of the husband she had left, but he was equally an enigma, his motives inexplicable. Which made him even more dangerous.

And the feelings he'd so effortlessly awoken in her—the longing to be touched as a woman, taken—would, in the end, lead only to disaster because there could be no lasting commitment from him either.

Caught up as she was in these mental struggles, she was suddenly jolted by the touch of his hand on her shoulder and rolled away from him with a gasp, remembering too late that her top was unfastened.

A wave of heated crimson swept up from her toes as she hastily covered her bare breasts with her hands, but Luca merely picked up her bikini bra and handed it to her without comment.

Once she was safely covered again, he said, glancing at the sky, 'It is becoming hotter than ever, so I suggest we look for somewhere with shade to have lunch.'

She took a deep breath, words of polite but resolute denial forming in her head that would finally and inexorably convince him he was wasting his time, only to hear herself say huskily, 'Yes—that seems a good idea.'

They chose a bar at the end of the promenade, sitting at a table under its striped awning to eat large prawns grilled on skewers accompanied by rice salad and fresh bread, and drink cold local beer. It was delicious, messy and relaxed in a way she wouldn't have dreamed it could be.

And he talked to her—asking her tastes in music, books, and the theatre. Making her laugh with his frankly cynical comments about the political situation. Seeking her views on topics like the global economy and climate change. Avoiding the questions she knew she would have found impossible to answer.

At the same time, at every moment, she was aware of his eyes on her, sometimes smiling, sometimes searching, always brilliant in their intensity. Aware of the proud lines of his nose and cheekbones—and how that lord-of-creation look softened when his mouth curved in amusement. Found herself watching him as if mesmerised. As if to gaze forever would not be enough.

Felt the ache of forbidden necessity deep within her. The helpless, shameful thrust of her hardening nipples against the confines of her bikini.

And when the meal was over, the bill paid, and Luca stood up, saying softly, 'Helen, *mia carissima*, I think it is time for a *siesta*,' she went with him willingly, her hand clasped in his, back to Casa Bianca. Her retreat. Her own very private space, shared with no-one. Until this moment.

Her hand shook as she tried to fit the key in the lock, and Luca took it from her and opened the door, then picked her up in his arms and lifted her over the threshold as if she was a bride.

Too late now to listen to the voice in her head telling her to step back because this was all wrong—so very wrong. That there could be no future with this man who was offering her only the transient pleasure of the moment. And—most of all— that she didn't do things like this—and never had. That there would be a price to be paid which she could not afford...

Then his lips took hers and the voice was silenced.

They were lying together on the bed, naked, in the warm golden light slanting across the bed from the shuttered window. The few clothes they'd been wearing had been tossed aside like leaves in a breeze as Luca had undressed her and then himself between kisses, his hands moving over her uncovered skin as if he was touching the delicate petals of a flower.

He pulled her closer, his kiss deepening as his tongue sought hers, thrusting into the sweetness of her mouth with sensual urgency, astonishing her with the swift glory of her response, her hands clasping his shoulders, twining round his neck, stroking his thick dark hair. Learning every smooth, supple line of him. Unable, it seemed, even in those first moments, to get enough of him as if a lifetime's waiting was ending at last.

Knowing, too, that, whatever pain still waited for her, there could be no turning back.

His hands moved downwards, his fingers moulding the swell of her breasts, teasing the rosy peaks to lift to the voluptuous caress of his mouth, making the breath sigh from her parted lips as he suckled her gently.

She had not known until now that her entire body could sing to the slow, languorous glide of a man's hands and lips exploring her. That there would be excitement to be discovered in the arch of her throat, the softness of her underarms and the inner hollow of her elbow. That his slow traverse of her spinal column would make her rear blindly against him, gasping, or that she would moan with pleasure as he cupped her small, firm buttocks and traced the slender line of her flanks.

But then no-one had touched her like this before, or whispered soft words of desire against the newly awakened eagerness of her untutored flesh.

Nor had she experienced the tip of a tongue seeking the whorls of her ear, or teeth nibbling gently at its lobe.

Her thighs had never parted, as they were doing now, welcoming the heated arousal of her lover's erection pressed between them. She reached down to find him, her fingertips stroking the silken length of the engorged male shaft in a kind of wonderment, as she felt his whole body quiver in responsive delight, making her realise that her need was shared—equalled.

And that it was too late to remind herself that it was only a temporary delight. That there could be no future in this. None.

His fingers were moving on her too, gently, exquisitely igniting new sensations, as he sought her tiny hidden pinnacle, bringing it to aching, swollen, delicious life, making her whimper, wordlessly, pleadingly against his shoulder as her body lifted to the delicate torment of his caress.

She was instantly aware of his touch changing, intensifying, drawing her inexorably into some blind, mindless region of the senses. Holding her there on an unknown brink for a breathless eternity before releasing her into a throbbing, soaring agony of pleasure.

And her body was still shaking from the last lingering tremors of rapture when he lifted himself over her, entering her, filling her with total completeness, then sliding his hands under her hips and raising her towards him in a silent command to lock her legs round his waist.

As he began to move slowly and rhythmically inside her, Ellie found herself remembering another time, another place, another man.

Recalling the feelings, the instincts she'd so deliberately denied herself then, but allowing them free rein now because it was all so incredibly, indescribably different.

Letting herself mirror every strong, powerful thrust, answering his demands with her own, her entire being alive and enthralled by the unexpected potential of her awakened sexuality. Feeling her inner muscles close round him then release. Hearing him groan in husky satisfaction at her response—at this mutual and glorious attuning of their bodies. Clinging to his sweat-slicked shoulders, as her mouth drank from his with eager, entranced delight.

I never dreamed… The only coherent thought that came to her as their bodies rose and fell together. *I never dreamed…*

Yet this was no dream. This was stark and beautiful reality, as inevitable as her next flurried breath. *What I was born for…*

Luca was moving faster now, driving more deeply into her hot, wet sheath, and Ellie could feel a strange, sweet tension building within her like a fist slowly clenching. A small, aching sound was forced from her throat as she stared up, eyes widening, at the man above her, dark against the sunlight, the sensations he was creating spiralling relentlessly out of control. Carrying her away on the scalding tide of his desire.

Then, as the first harsh spasm tore through her and she dissolved into shuddering helpless ecstasy, she cried out, her voice breaking on his name and heard him answer her.

CHAPTER ELEVEN

WHEN THE WORLD finally stopped reeling, Ellie found she was lying in his arms, her head pillowed on his chest, as he gently stroked the damp hair back from her forehead. There were a thousand questions teeming in her mind, but the warm aftermath of passion was being superseded by a sudden agony of shyness at the memory of her abandoned surrender, and she knew she could ask none of them.

He must have sensed her growing tension because he said softly, 'Is all well with you, *mia bella*? I did not—hurt you?'

'No—oh, no.' She hesitated then said on a little rush of words, 'I just—didn't realise—didn't know...'

'And now that you do?' He tilted her chin, raising her face for his kiss. Caressing her lips with his until she relaxed back into his embrace. 'You have no regrets I hope?'

'No,' Ellie said slowly. 'I'll never have those—whatever happens.'

'Even when I have to leave you?' His hand slid down to clasp the curve of her hip.

There was a heartbeat of silence, then she said, 'Are you planning to go?'

'At some moment, *sì*.' There was a smile in his voice. '*Naturalmente*, I have to return to my hotel to change my clothes, *mia cara*, in order to take you to dinner.' He kissed her again. 'But not immediately,' he murmured against her lips, his hand moving with quiet purpose.

'No,' she whispered back. 'Not immediately.' And gave

herself up to the renewed joy of his touch. The slow delicious establishment of a need as passionate as it was mutual. A reaching out to each other that somehow transcended the purely physical, as it carried them to the sweet agony of orgasm, and as Ellie rested in its honeyed aftermath, she realised there were tears on her face.

Afterwards, she made coffee, black and strong, and as she carried the cups into the living room, she found him, fresh from the shower, a towel draped round his hips, studying her laptop and the files beside it.

He turned to look at her, his slow smile reminding her of what had just happened between them under the warm cascade of water, and a wave of heat enveloped her.

'You work here?' His brows lifted.

'Of course.' Ellie kept her tone light. 'Just as I would in any other place. I have my living to earn.'

'Ah, yes,' he said softly. 'And you do—what precisely?'

'I translate from English for a publishing house called Avortino.'

'Love stories, *mia bella*?' His tone teased her.

Ellie shook her head. 'Nothing like that. Mostly non-fiction. Often quite technical stuff.' She opened the top file and handed him a couple of pages. 'You see?'

He drew her to him, his arm lightly round her waist, and read, grimacing slightly. 'You find this—interesting?'

'Not this particular assignment perhaps. But, on the whole, it's a job I love,' she said. *And it demands a high level of concentration—something which has proved a lifeline in the past and may do so again.*

She added quietly, 'In future, I may go back to working in-house. I haven't quite decided yet.'

'No,' he said softly. 'In your situation, there must be so many decisions to be made.'

As well as many more that will be made for me…

He drank his coffee, and put down the cup. 'Now, I must go.' He picked up his discarded clothes still lying with hers on the floor, mute evidence of how eagerly they'd stripped each other as soon as the front door closed behind them.

As he dropped his towel, Ellie moved closer, running a tantalising finger down the length of his strong spine. 'Do you have to—really?' she whispered.

He grinned at her over his shoulder. '*Si, carissima*. We have to eat, *dopo tutto* and I think even Santino would draw the line if we arrived tonight like this.' He caught his breath as her hand strayed lower. 'However, the sooner I leave, my little witch, the sooner I shall return. And after we have eaten, we shall have the entire night to please each other so do not tempt me now.'

'You mean I could?'

He dragged on his shorts, zipped them and turned to pull her into his arms. 'Always,' he muttered unevenly against her lips.

Alone, Ellie pressed a hand to the soft tingle of her mouth, aware that her entire body was aglow, singing with fulfilment.

I'm a different person, she thought wonderingly. I've been re-born—and nothing will ever be the same again.

And she whispered his name, yearningly, achingly, into the silence.

But it can't last…

That was what Ellie had to keep telling herself, over and over again as each blissful day and night slid past and a measure of sanity began to return. It just can't…

However warm and passionate it might be, however sweet the madness, it was still only an interlude. It had no future and when the real world intervened again, which at some point it must, she would have to learn to be alone again.

Even the mark on her finger where her wedding ring had been had now faded as if it had never existed—rather, she thought, like the marriage itself. A few months that had involved a different lifetime and a different girl. A place to which she could never return. A time for her to begin her life again.

Once or twice Ellie had wished that she still had some of the designer clothes and sexy lingerie that had filled the closets at Vostranto, so that she could wow him when he arrived to pick her up each evening.

On the other hand, as she reminded herself, none of those glamorous garments had done much for her in the past, so instead she'd visited Porto Vecchio's only boutique and bought herself a new and very inexpensive dress, in a soft and floating fabric with dark green flowers on a cream background, and watched with delight his face light up when he saw her.

'How very lovely you are,' he'd whispered as he kissed her, his hands sensuous as they moulded her slender shape through the thin material. Making them, as she recalled, very late for dinner even by Italian standards.

Although they spent most of their waking hours—as well as the time they slept—together, he had never asked if he might move out of the hotel and join her at Casa Bianca as she'd half-expected, and Ellie had hesitated to suggest it herself. After all, it was hardly a necessity, she thought, when they were so happy with life just as it was.

Also, it seemed that he had totally accepted her need to work because he never intruded on her after he'd left for the hotel each morning, generally timing his return for around noon. It occurred to her that perhaps he also had matters to attend to in the interim period, although he never mentioned them directly.

All that, she thought, savoured too much of the real world rather than the idyll they were sharing, and maybe he thought so too.

The warm weather continued, drawing them each afternoon to the beach and the shade of their rock, usually accompanied by Poco. The Signora was clearly intrigued by her young neighbour's new human companion, her eyes twinkling at him in undisguised appreciation, but she nobly forbore to ask any questions. And if she saw him leave in the early mornings, it was never mentioned.

When, at last, she did sound a note of caution, it concerned the weather rather than personal relationships.

'No more beautiful days.' She peered at the sky frowning. 'Tomorrow, or perhaps tonight there will be rain. Perhaps a storm.'

'Oh,' Ellie said, dismayed. 'I hope you're wrong.'

'Never,' the Signora exclaimed superbly. She pressed a dramatic fist to the shelf of her bosom. 'I know this place the whole of my life. I know how quickly things can change. So make the most of today, Elena, because it cannot last.'

And as Ellie walked back to Casa Bianca, she heard the echo of her own inner warnings, and felt herself shiver as if the threatened rain had already begun to fall.

By evening, the clouds were already gathering and a chilly wind had sprung up making the candle-flames dance and flicker under their glass shades at the *trattoria*.

'The Signora was right,' Ellie said as they ate their chicken *puttanesca*. 'All good things do come to an end.'

He took her hand, and she saw him looking down at her bare wedding finger. He said quietly, 'But other things can take their place.'

She said with faint breathlessness, 'Perhaps I don't want anything to change.'

'Yet I think it must.' His voice was gentle. 'Because we cannot continue as we are. Surely you see that.'

'Yes.' She withdrew her hand from his clasp. 'Yes, I do. I—I accept that totally. I mean—when you came down here, you can't have foreseen or planned for this to happen. For us to meet as we did.'

'No,' he said. 'You are right. I did not anticipate—any of it.'

'And if you'd simply stayed in your hotel like most of the other guests, it would have been entirely different.'

'I cannot deny that either.' He picked up his glass and drank, the movement jerky.

She looked down at the table. 'So I need you to know that I—I didn't expect it either.'

His mouth twisted. 'As you made clear, *mia cara*. You were not easy to convince.'

'Then let me make this clear too.' She took a deep breath. 'I don't expect nor want anything more either.'

He was silent for a moment. 'You cannot mean that,' he said at last. 'Are you saying these things because of the past? Because of your marriage—the way it was?'

'I'm saying that we have our real lives—our actual commitments—far away from here.' She lifted her chin. 'We've had this—time together, these few days and nights, and they've been wonderful, but that's all. There's nothing else, and there never can be.'

She paused. 'So maybe a change now is appropriate, even necessary. Isn't there a saying—quit while you're ahead?'

'I have heard it used,' he said slowly. 'But is that truly what you wish?'

'Yes, *signore*.' Her gaze met his without wavering. 'It is.'

But I'm lying, she thought, pain twisting inside her. I want to hear you tell me that in spite of everything, we have a future. I want you to say that you love me. I wish for the impossible.

And, instead, saw him glance towards the window, hit by the first spatter of drops.

He said lightly, 'It seems that, in any case, we will not be going to the beach tomorrow. What will Poco do?'

'Stay indoors with the Signora.' She made her tone match his, carefully masking the agony of loss. 'He loves going in the sea, but he hates the rain. He doesn't seem to recognise that they're both water.'

He even managed to look amused. 'Well, he is not alone in that, *mia cara*.' He paused. 'Have you always liked dogs?'

'We had a golden retriever when I was a child.' She drank some wine. From somewhere managed to produce a reminiscent smile. 'He was called Benji, and he was big and soft and sweet.' She added with faint huskiness, 'I missed him terribly when he died.'

And this—this is like another death...

'He was not replaced?'

She shook her head. 'It wasn't possible. My father had a new job and we were moving to an apartment without a garden.'

'Che peccato,' he said. He leaned back in his chair, surveying her with narrowed eyes. 'I am trying to imagine,' he said, 'how you looked when you were a little girl.'

Oh God, don't do this to me—please.

She shrugged. 'Scrawny. Hair in plaits. Big eyes.' She grimaced. 'Only the hairstyle has really changed.'

He gave a despairing glance at the ceiling. *'Dio mio,* how many times do I need to say how beautiful you are before you believe me?'

At least once a day, she thought, for the rest of my life. One of so many things I can never tell you in return.

Santino lent them an ancient umbrella for the walk back to the Casa Bianca, its shelter precarious as the wind threatened to turn it inside out.

At the door, she halted. 'Perhaps we should say *"Addio"* here.'

'A clean break?' he queried derisively. 'No, *mia bella.* Never in this world.'

And as he had done that first time, he unlocked the door himself, carrying her into the house. Once inside, he put her on her feet and stood for a long moment, looking down into her face.

She tried again. 'Believe me, please. This—is so unwise.'

'I agree,' he said. 'But it is also far too late for wisdom.'

He took her gently in his arms and began to kiss her slowly and very deeply, his mouth moving on hers in insistent demand, making her moan softly with the aching need of arousal before he lifted her again, shouldering his way into the bedroom.

His hands were deft as he undressed her, his mouth tender and seeking on her uncovered body and she held him, hands clasping his shoulders, offering herself for his possession, gasping a little as he filled her and made her complete. As they moved together in the unison that they had learned, knowing every nuance of each other's responses.

Yet even as she began to dissolve into delight, Ellie could feel that he was holding back, concentrating on her pleasure, her satisfaction rather than his own. But it was too late for protest or to lure him into equal abandonment because her senses were already spiralling giddily out of control, her body shuddering in the first fierce spasms of climax.

And even after she had cried out, her voice lost and wondering, he had not finished with her, his lips performing a sensuous traverse down the length of her trembling sweat-dampened body, his hand parting her thighs for the voluptuous caress of his fingers and his tongue.

She tried to tell him that it was too soon—that it was impossible—but she couldn't speak, caught once more in the irresistible rush of desire. Carried away almost inexorably. Convulsed—drained by its culmination.

He said her name hoarsely and took her again, his strong body driving her to limits she'd never guessed at. Urging her towards some dangerous edge and holding her there for a breathless, agonised eternity before permitting them both the harsh, pulsating tumult of release.

Sated, exhausted, Ellie lay beneath him, treasuring the relaxed weight of his body against hers, stroking the dark head pillowed on her breasts.

The calm, she thought, after the storm. Then, hearing the rattle of the wind against the shutters and the low rumble of thunder in the distance, she thought of all the other storms still to come. And how they could so easily tear her life apart.

And wondered how she would ever bear it.

It was just after dawn when she woke with a start, and sat up, wondering what had disturbed her. And in that same moment, discovered she was alone.

At first, she remained still, listening intently for the sound of the shower, trying to detect the aroma of coffee in the air. Searching for the normality of morning, but there was nothing.

And as her eyes grew accustomed to the dimness of the room, she saw that his clothes were missing too.

Ellie bit her lip, tasting blood. She wasn't accustomed to this, she thought. She'd become used to waking in his arms, his warm mouth coaxing her to desire. Later, to showering with him, running her fingers laughingly over the stubble on his chin and the faint marks it had left on her skin.

Yet at some moment, it seemed, he'd decided that a clean break was best after all. And gone. Without a kiss. Without a word.

She flung back the covers and got up, reaching for her robe. With last night's memories crowding in on her—his hands, his lips, the scent, the taste of him—it was impossible to stay where she was, or try to sleep again.

In the living room, she paused, looking round her in a kind of desperation. This little house—her refuge for so long—suddenly felt bleak and empty, as if it no longer belonged to her, but to some stranger. As if the heart had been ripped out of it. Or was it the dark hollow that had opened up inside herself that she was sensing?

She took a deep, steadying breath, then padded into the kitchen and put the coffee to brew, before toasting some bread to go with the ham and cheese she'd taken from the fridge for breakfast.

Knowing she needed to keep herself occupied far more than she required food.

She ate what she could, then showered and dressed in denim jeans and a dark blue sweater, grimacing at the pallid face which looked back at her from the mirror.

She sat down at her work table with gritted teeth, but her usual ability to concentrate had deserted her. She found she was staring at the rain-lashed window, wondering where he was, what he was doing, what he was thinking. Then endlessly repeating everything that had been said between them the previous night. Telling herself as she did so that she had done absolutely the right thing. That she hadn't cried or begun a sentence with 'Can't we…' so that at least she could emerge from this extraordinary situation with some semblance of dignity.

And one day she'd be able to look back and be proud—maybe even glad that she'd had the strength to behave so well.

At last, she gave up on the current translation, and deciding that struggling against the wind and rain was better than fighting her unhappy thoughts, she took the ancient hooded waterproof cape that had once belonged to her grandmother from the cupboard, and went for a walk.

Under the leaden sky, a grey sea hurled foam-tipped waves at the beach, the hiss and roar of its ebb competing with the noisy gusts that whipped at Ellie's cape, and stung her face with whipped up particles of sand.

Head bent, she battled along the deserted promenade, her imagination telling her that at any moment she would hear him say her name—her real name—and she would look up and see him there, on his way to find her and say all the things she longed to hear.

Last night in the *trattoria* she'd let fear and pride get the better of her, but now there was only her need for him. Her longing to be his in any way he wanted. However little he could offer.

She stopped, gazing up at the bulk of the hotel above her on the headland, determination building inside her. What she was planning was probably the height of stupidity, but, as he'd said last night, it was too late for wisdom.

I have to see him, she thought. Even now. Talk to him. I can't let it end like this—not without knowing—being certain…

She made for the long, steep flight of steps cut into the cliff, and began to climb. When she reached the top, breathless and dishevelled, she cut across the gardens to the hotel's main entrance, and the wide glass doors opened at her approach.

The foyer was almost empty, but there was a buzz of laughter and chatter from the bar where the guests were enjoying their pre-lunch drinks.

Ellie went straight across the wide expanse of marble floor to the reception desk, water dripping from her cape. A man in a formal dark suit raised his eyes from the computer screen he was scanning and stared at her as if he could not believe the presence of such a scarecrow in the hotel's sophisticated surroundings.

He said with hauteur, 'I may help you, *signorina?*'

Pushing back her hood, she said quietly, 'I wish to speak to Count Manzini, if you please. I believe he is staying here.'

'He was a guest, *signorina*, but no longer.' The man offered a thin smile. 'He left two hours ago to return to Rome.'

The world seemed suddenly to recede to a great distance. Ellie leaned against the edge of the desk. She said, 'I didn't realise he was leaving so soon. Did he say—why?'

She received a disparaging look. 'His Excellency gave no reason for his departure, *signorina*. He is not obliged to explain himself. But I believe he received a telephone call.'

'I see.' Ellie paused. 'Do you know if he is planning to come back?'

'He did not say so, *signorina*. He was clearly in a hurry to be gone.'

Ellie lifted her chin. 'Well, I'm sorry to have missed him, but no doubt we'll meet up when I too return to Rome.'

'*Indubbiamente, signorina.*' He inclined his head with insincere courtesy. 'Is there any other way in which I can assist you?'

'No,' she said. 'Thank you. I should also have telephoned instead of wasting a journey.'

As she walked back towards the entrance, she realised that her legs were shaking and prayed it did not show. She did not dare risk the steps again, but made her way carefully down the winding hill, half dizzy with the questions teeming in her mind.

As she reached Casa Bianca, the Signora's door opened, and the good woman appeared under an umbrella, brandishing an envelope. 'This came for you, *cara*.' She gave her a shrewd look. 'A boy was knocking at your door—a *fattorino* from the hotel, I think.'

The envelope was cream, thick and expensive, bearing the single word 'Elena'.

'*Grazie.*' Ellie forced a smile and took the letter into her own house to the Signora's evident disappointment. She removed her cape and hung it in the shower to dry, then sat down and opened the envelope.

'Circumstances force my return to the city,' the letter began abruptly. 'And perhaps it is better this way, even though so much still remains unsaid between us.

'You were right, of course. I did not come to Porto Vecchio in order to become your lover. On the contrary, my original purpose was to agree terms for the separation you requested when you left Vostranto.

'I allowed myself to become sidetracked, but the ridiculous pretence, which should never have begun, is now over. Luca and Helen no longer exist, and should be forgotten. I accept too that the marriage between us is over.

'In conclusion, let me say that I intend to make full financial provision for you in the divorce settlement, and you may use this or not as you wish.

'This will be a matter for discussion at our next meeting.'

His signature 'Angelo' was a dark slash at the foot of the page, and Ellie felt the anger in it like a slap across the face.

She sat staring down at the words in all their bitterness and finality until the tears she could not hold back made them first blur and, eventually, vanish altogether as she wept for everything that might have been, but was now lost forever.

CHAPTER TWELVE

RIDICULOUS PRETENCE...

Those were the words which haunted Ellie for the rest of the day, and the greater part of the night.

Of course that was all it had been, she told herself over and over again. She'd known that from the first, but, somehow, she'd allowed herself to forget for a while. To let herself be drawn into this crazy charade that he'd initiated. And, almost, in some incredible way, come to believe it.

To actually think that Angelo Luca Manzini was the lover she'd only dared to imagine in her wildest dreams. And, in the most dangerous kind of wishful thinking, to suppose that some of these dreams might even come true.

Just how many kinds of a fool was it possible to be? she wondered in quiet anguish as she contemplated what she had done. What she had allowed him to do.

After all, she knew that he didn't care for her—that it was Silvia he really wanted. That evening at the reception, she'd seen with her own eyes that, in spite of everything, the passion still burned as brightly as ever between them.

Dear God, wasn't it the knowledge of that, with all its attendant humiliation, that had made her leave Vostranto? Leave him, as she'd thought, forever?

Yet, somehow, he'd made her think she was beautiful—desirable—when all the time he'd simply been amusing himself. Or, which was even worse, perhaps taking his revenge for all those past rejections of his lovemaking.

Making a deliberate nonsense of her avowed indifference to him. Demonstrating that she was just the same as any of the other women who'd shared his bed. As easy to seduce. As easy to walk away from when he wished it to end.

And he had wished it, she reminded herself painfully, as she read once more the letter that she already knew by heart. He'd come to Porto Vecchio to offer her a divorce—the first one in the entire history of the Manzini family and bound to set tongues wagging in conjecture all over Rome.

But giving her the freedom she'd asked for was no simple act of altruism on his part, she reminded herself stonily. He had his own reasons for wanting their sham of a marriage to end, no matter what scandal that might provoke.

She had little doubt that Silvia was one of the topics for discussion still not touched upon, and she could only be thankful to have been spared the pain of that. Because her cousin had to be the motivation driving him to seek his liberation, no matter what the consequences.

That, she thought wretchedly, and the fact that I've totally failed to give him the child he asked from me.

She remembered Silvia standing greedy-eyed in the bedroom at Vostranto, already planning the change in her future. Supremely confident in her beauty, and the power of her sexuality to win Angelo back. To become the Countess Manzini as she'd always intended.

Between the two of them, they've wrecked my life, Ellie thought, pain wrenching at her heart. And I can't deal with that rationally. It's impossible.

And yet, having come all this way, making this specific journey in order to administer the *coup de grâce*, some obscure passing whim had caused him to postpone his decision. Instead, hiding behind other names, other identities, in the process messing with her head and destroying her power to reason or to be on her guard as she should have been, Angelo had played his own private game with her.

A game that was now over.

But at least she had not given him the opportunity to finish it. The moment he'd hinted that they could not continue as they were, she'd acted swiftly, decisively. She could always be proud of that if nothing else. Proud that she hadn't waited for sentence to be pronounced.

And if she'd changed her mind a short while later and gone to find him—well, he would never, ever know that she'd yielded to such pathetic weakness. Or be aware that, without him, she felt only half alive, pacing the floor since his departure, unable to settle or think of anything but him.

She'd stripped the bed and re-made it so that there would be no lingering trace of the cologne he used to act as a reminder of his presence tempting her to reach for him across the empty space beside her.

But, as she soon discovered, it made little difference, because he was not just in the bedroom, but everywhere.

She found him in the shower, stroking scented gel into her skin. At the stove in the kitchen, creating the best carbonara sauce she'd ever tasted to go with the pasta. In the living room, sharing the old sofa with her, his hands and lips caressing her in the preliminaries to love, before pulling her, laughing, down on to the soft rug for his possession.

She couldn't even stand at the sink without recalling how he would appear behind her, his arms sliding round her waist as he pushed her hair away in order to nuzzle the nape of her neck.

Forcing her to the realisation that the freedom she'd demanded was just another illusion. That in her heart and mind she was still chained to him. And that her precious Casa Bianca was no longer a sanctuary but a prison.

She tried to pinpoint the time—the day—the hour when she had begun to want him, aware that it was well before she'd admitted as much to herself, ashamed to recognise how long ago it truly was. Certainly before the living nightmare of her marriage had been imposed on her.

I was like a child crying for the moon, she acknowledged sadly, knowing full well that it was unattainable. That I was still just as I'd always been—Silvia Alberoni's younger, plainer cousin.

Yet, I built every possible defence I could against him. Insisted he keep his distance. Threw myself into work as if my life depended on it. Tried desperately not to wonder where he was and who he might be with when he stayed in Rome. Fought each lift of the heart when he returned to Vostranto, each quiver of the senses when I was alone with him and all the other small, secret self-betrayals in case he picked them up on some inner male radar and guessed the truth.

And then I ran away, believing I was escaping from the humiliation of being set aside as the failed, unwanted wife. Thinking I could somehow avoid a broken heart. When it was here waiting for me all the time.

Oh, why did he have to follow me? Why couldn't he have left it all in the hands of his lawyers?

Even after another three days she was unable to find answers to those or any of the other questions tormenting her, enclosing her in a kind of limbo.

On the surface, her life went on as usual. She forced herself back to work, relying on her strict professionalism to get her through her assignments.

The weather was still blustery, but fine enough to enable her to escape at some point from the four walls that used to be her safeguard. She took Poco for long walks, evading the Signora's coy queries about 'the return of your handsome friend'.

At the *trattoria*, which she continued to brave each evening, Santino and Maria were more discreet, but she could sense their brimming curiosity too—and their disappointment.

On the morning of the fourth day, she had just cleared away breakfast and was on her way to her laptop, when there was a loud rap at the front door.

Her heart seemed to lurch, and for a stunned instant, she stood staring across the room, aware what she was hoping and despising herself for it.

A second impatient knock and a rattle at the door handle prompted her into action, reaching for her keys.

She flung the door open, her lips parting in a soundless gasp as she saw who was waiting for her.

'So you are here.' Silvia walked past her into the living room. 'I had begun to wonder.' She began to unbutton her white trench coat. 'Aren't you going to ask me to sit down, *cara*? Offer me coffee? I am sure I can smell some.'

Ellie remained where she was. She said quietly, 'Why have you come here?'

Silvia's eyes widened in assumed surprise. 'But, Elena *mia*, to talk to you, of course. To deal with the kind of detail that men somehow find so difficult.' She shrugged. 'But let us examine the broad picture first. You have, of course, agreed that your marriage to Angelo is finally and irretrievably over.'

Ellie said stonily, 'I think that is my business and his. No-one else's.'

'On the contrary, as the other person most nearly involved in this, I have a right to know what is planned. And to help the matter reach a rapid and satisfactory conclusion.' She draped her coat over the arm of the sofa, and sat down, crossing her legs. 'I presume this is also your wish.'

Ellie walked over to the table and leaned against it, the hard, polished edge biting into her hands. 'And what about Ernesto?' she queried tautly. 'Does he have a view in all this?'

Silvia examined her nails. 'Of course, shut away in this forgotten corner, you cannot know what is happening in the wide world. Let me enlighten you. Ernesto and I are no longer together and will very soon be divorced.'

'How convenient,' Ellie returned bitingly.

Silvia laughed. 'More of a necessity, *cara*, once he had heard the news. When I told him I was having Angelo's child. Even he knew then he could not keep me with him.'

Ellie's heart seemed to have stopped beating. She stared at Silvia, knowing she would never be able to forget the triumph in the glowing eyes, or the faint mocking smile that curved her cousin's mouth.

She said in a voice she didn't recognise, 'I don't believe you.'

'You mean because in the past I have never been drawn to the idea of having babies?' Silvia nodded. 'It is true. I admit it.' She paused. 'But who should know better than you, Elena, how much Angelo needs an heir? And I have come to realise that, when you love a man, you wish to give him everything he wants.' Her smile widened. 'So that is what I have done, and you cannot imagine his delight.'

Ellie looked down at the floor, biting the inside of her lip until she tasted blood. Fighting one pain with another.

'Naturally we wish to be married as soon as possible,' Silvia went on brightly. 'So I suggested that Angelo should come down here in person and talk to you. Put his powers of persuasion to good use rather than issue an ultimatum from a distance. When his heart is set on a thing, he becomes quite impossible to resist, don't you find?

'And as he is now instructing his lawyers, his methods were clearly successful.' She gave a little gurgle of laughter. 'He has always believed that the end justifies the means and I understand he had you eating out of the palm of his hand.'

She paused again. 'But we now feel that for his grandmother's sake—and to spare Madrina's feelings too—it would be better if your marriage was quietly annulled. After all, *cara*, neither of you wished to marry the other, so it should be quite simple to arrange.'

'I know very little of these things.' Ellie was astonished to hear the steadiness of her own voice. 'But I'll sign whatever paperwork is necessary, if that's what you came to hear. And now I'd like you to go.'

Silvia rose unhurriedly, smoothing her skirt. 'You seem a little disturbed, *cara*.' Her gaze searched her cousin's white face. 'The situation is awkward, perhaps, but there is no real need for embarrassment between us. Whatever Angelo felt obliged to do was for my sake and the sake of our future together. I know this, so please believe that I do not begrudge the time he spent with you, or how it was spent. And I wish you well.'

Ellie did not reply. Somehow she managed to get to the door without stumbling, and hold it open for her unwanted visitor. Somehow, she managed to close it and lock it behind her.

Then she bolted to the bathroom and was instantly and violently sick.

'You are selling Casa Bianca?' The Signora stared at Ellie in disbelief. 'Your grandmother's house where you have known such happiness for so long? No, it is impossible. You could not do such a thing.'

'I'm afraid that I must.' Ellie gave her neighbour a strained smile. 'Coming here for all these years has been wonderful, but nothing lasts forever, and my life is going to be very different from now on. In fact I'm probably going to get a job in England and live there, so it—it's time to sell.'

She added, 'Someone from the property company is coming to give a valuation this afternoon. I wanted to tell you myself before he arrived.'

'But why—why do you do this? Italy is your home. Your friends are here. Also your family.'

Ellie winced inwardly. 'But I'm going to find another home, somewhere else. I—I need to make a change. I've been thinking about it for a while.'

'I know this while,' the Signora said darkly. 'It is since your handsome man went away. You cannot deceive me, Elena.' She made an impassioned gesture. 'So if he comes back, and you are no longer here—what then? How will he find you?'

Ellie took a deep breath. 'There's no question of that. I have my own life to deal with. No-one else is involved.'

'But you were happy with him,' the Signora said gently. 'All the world could see it. Now it is different—as if a light inside you has gone out.' She paused. 'And there will be sadness here too. You will be much missed by myself and many others. Poco will grieve.'

Ellie bent to fondle the little dog's ears. 'Perhaps your new neighbours will like walking too,' she whispered to him.

Detaching herself would not be easy, Ellie thought when she was back in her own living room. But it had to be done. She could neither stay here nor return to Rome.

She had to find some other place where she could hide until the wounds Silvia had so contemptuously inflicted had healed. Somewhere her cousin would never find. Or Angelo either…

Our next meeting…

It was those casual words from his letter, now torn up and burned, which had forced this drastic action from her. Because the thought of having to see him again, even briefly in the formality of a lawyer's office, was totally, and hideously unbearable.

His betrayal of her was worse than she could ever have imagined, leaving her hollow with pain and shock. It was also incomprehensible because he already knew from the note she'd left she was willing to divorce him. There was no need for any extra 'persuasion' from him with or without Silvia's sanction, so why had he gone to those lengths to seduce her? To lure her into a fantasy world and pretend such tenderness—such desire. She shuddered, her throat tightening with renewed misery. It was cynical, wicked, unforgivable.

But the person she most needed to forgive was herself—for allowing it to happen. For letting him indulge his sexual ego at her expense.

If he'd needed to make sure she'd meant what she said, why hadn't he been honest with her—told her that he had resumed his affair with her cousin and that Silvia was pregnant? It would have hurt terribly, but it would hardly have been any great surprise. A blow she'd been expecting to fall. Besides, the raw and monstrous pain now tearing her apart was far worse.

Yet that was not her only torment. Because even hating him as she did—as she must do—could not confer any kind of immunity from him. On the contrary, she had to face the humiliating truth that she dared not risk another confrontation. That her anger and misery over his treachery might not be sufficient protection. That if he smiled at her, moved towards her or—dear God—touched her, she might not be able to trust herself to turn away.

She needed another refuge and fast. A place where no-one would dream of looking for her. Not Nonna Cosima, Madrina or even Tullia, she thought with a pang. And once they learned the reason for her sudden disappearance, as they soon would, none of them could really blame her.

A place where she would be safe, she told herself with a sigh. And where she might one day forget that she was also running from herself.

'And they lived happily ever after.' The story drawn to its proper conclusion, Ellie closed her book and smiled down at the semi-circle of entranced faces in front of her.

'More, *signorina*, more,' a chorus of small voices petitioned, but she shook her head.

'It is almost time for the lunch bell. If you are late, Mother Felicitas might say there must be no more stories.'

However far-fetched the threat, the children accepted it and trooped off.

Ellie slid the book into her bag, and rose, preparing to follow them, then paused, walking instead to the sunlit window. It was a wonderful view of rolling green hills, shimmering in the haze of summer heat, interspersed with fields of yellow mustard and scarlet poppies. The nearest town was a mere smudge on the horizon.

Directly below was a small paved courtyard with a mulberry tree, its canopy shading a wooden seat, which had become one of Ellie's favourite places.

The convent was the perfect sanctuary, she thought. And she would never be able to sufficiently repay Mother Felicitas for offering it to her. Or for asking so few questions.

When Ellie had told her haltingly that her marriage was over, she had simply expressed quiet concern. And she had also acceded to Ellie's request that no-one should be informed of her presence—with one proviso.

'I understand that you need time and privacy to consider your future, my dear child, and they are yours. But if anyone asks me directly at any point if you are with us here, I will not lie.'

Ellie bent her head. 'That—won't happen.'

Nor had it. Six weeks before, while she was still at Casa Bianca, she had written to both Angelo's grandmother and the Principessa stating that she was well and happy but needed to be alone, and asking them to understand and not worry about her.

Her room in the part of the convent that housed the orphanage and school was pleasant if a little Spartan, its bed too narrow to encourage forbidden dreams.

On the practical side, Mother Felicitas had arranged an extra table and chair so that she could continue to work as usual. She paid for her board and lodging, but in addition she helped out in the school, giving informal English lessons to some of the older children and reading her own translations of popular children's stories to the younger ones.

Her mail was being sent on by arrangement from the property company selling her house in Porto Vecchio, but so far there was no sign of the documentation which would begin the legal dissolution of her marriage.

Clearly Angelo's lawyers did not share Silvia's sense of urgency about the procedure, thought Ellie who found the delay bewildering. Apart from anything else, surely Angelo's pride would demand his heir should be born in wedlock.

She found the whole situation becoming seriously unsettling. How could she begin again, or even plan positively for the future, with this cloud still hanging over her?

In spite of the convent's almost tangible air of peace, the strain of waiting was taking its physical toll of her. The food was good and plentiful, but her appetite had temporarily deserted her, and she had lost a little weight. She felt weary much of the time too, yet had trouble sleeping. In addition, and not too surprisingly, she found herself often on the verge of tears. She'd taken her troubles apologetically to the Infirmarian,

Sister Perpetua who, in her quiet noncommittal way, had recommended fresh air and exercise.

She'd followed her advice, yet, this morning, she'd woken with a slight headache and vague queasiness as if she was coming down with a virus.

I can't afford to be ill, she told herself. I've too much else to cope with, and I don't want to be a liability to the nuns either.

Being with the children had lifted her as it invariably did, and the headache at least had faded. But the thought of food was totally unappealing, Ellie admitted with a sigh, resting her forehead against the glass. Maybe she would forget the mid-day meal and rest on her bed for a while.

As she turned from the window, Mother Felicitas came into the room, an envelope in her hand.

'This came for you, dear child.'

It was from the property company in Porto Vecchio, Ellie saw listlessly. Perhaps they'd sold Casa Bianca, which would be gratifying, of course, but still wasn't the news she was expecting.

She slit open the envelope and extracted the single sheet, scanning the typewritten contents.

There had been, she read, a lot of interest in Casa Bianca, but they had accepted on her behalf an excellent cash offer well above the asking price from Count Angelo Manzini.

Ellie gave a gasp, her hand straying to her lips as the words swam in front of her incredulous gaze. She turned to Mother Felicitas. Her voice barely audible, she said, 'My home. He's bought my home—for her...' and felt herself slide down into impenetrable darkness.

CHAPTER THIRTEEN

'THERE'S NOTHING WRONG with me,' Ellie protested. 'I shouldn't be in the Infirmary. I—I just had a shock, that's all, and that's why I fainted. I—I'm not ill.'

'No, no.' Mother Felicitas patted her hand. 'Sister Perpetua assures me that the symptoms of early pregnancy are often uncomfortable, but only rarely do they become serious.'

If a bomb had gone off in the quiet Infirmary, Ellie could not have been more horrified.

When she could speak: 'A baby? She says I'm having a baby? But I can't be. It's impossible.'

'She nursed in an obstetrics hospital before she joined our Order,' Mother Felicitas said gently. 'She told me what she suspected over a week ago.' She paused. 'Whatever has happened in the past, Contessa, this is news that you must share with your husband.'

'No.' Ellie sat up, icy with sudden alarm. 'I can't do that.'

'But you may carry the heir to an important name, my child. This cannot remain a secret. Count Manzini has to know he is to be a father.'

'That's the last thing he'll want to hear,' Ellie whispered. 'Please believe me, Reverend Mother, and don't ask me to explain.' And as the realisation of everything she had lost overwhelmed her, she began to weep silently and hopelessly.

Worn out emotionally, she slept better that night, aided by a tisana of Sister Perpetua's making, and woke the next day calmer, and filled with a new sense of resolution.

She would close her mind to the past, and use the money that Angelo had paid to take Casa Bianca from her to fund her new life in England.

He had everything now, she thought, pain twisting inside her. Her pride, her memories, her little house—and the love— the need she'd tried desperately to deny, and which he had also taken so carelessly, because he could.

At lunchtime, she made herself eat a bowl of soup and a little pasta, then, encouraged by Sister Perpetua, went to sit out under the mulberry tree. It was a hot, drowsy day with little breeze when even the birdsong seemed muted, and not ideal, she thought wryly, for the making of serious plans. For looking forward instead of back as she must do.

And at first, when she heard the excited yapping of a dog disturbing the stillness, Ellie thought she must be having a waking dream.

But bundling across the courtyard towards her was total reality with a round face and drooping ears, his tail wagging furiously and his barking changing to squeaks of excitement.

She jerked upright, staring in disbelief. 'Poco?' she whispered. 'Poco, what are you doing here?'

And then she realised who was following him, standing in the archway, tall and lean in cream denim pants and a black polo shirt, watching her in silence.

Oh, no, she wailed inwardly. It can't be true. This can't be happening to me.

She knew what she must look like—washed out with scared eyes and lank hair in a faded cotton dress—and as she jumped to her feet, she folded her arms defensively across her body.

Angelo halted, brows lifting almost resignedly as he saw the gesture. He said quietly, '*Buona sera*, Elena. *Come sta?*'

'I was all right,' she said. 'Until now.'

He was thinner, she thought with a wrench of the heart, the lines of the dark face more clearly marked, his eyes shadowed, his mouth bleaker. But she could not let herself see these things. Feel the ache of them.

She said tautly, 'I'm told you've bought Casa Bianca. If you mean it as a gift for Silvia, you've wasted your money. She never liked Porto Vecchio even as a child. She always preferred places with glitz and glamour.'

'I bought it for myself,' he said. 'Do you wish to know why?'

'I presume because it's a way of providing for me that I can't refuse. But it doesn't really matter.' She lifted her chin. 'The house is gone, and soon I shall be gone too.'

She paused. 'So, how did you find me? Did Mother Felicitas contact you—even though she promised...?'

'No,' he said. 'She did not. No-one did. I saw some mail on a desk at the property company addressed to the Daughters of the Nativity, and remembered that I'd seen you talking to Mother Felicitas at that last reception we'd attended together.'

His mouth twisted. 'Suddenly, after all the fruitless days and weeks of searching, everything fell into place. So, I came here asking for you, and she sent me here.'

Poco was lying on his back at Ellie's feet, waving ecstatic paws in the air and she knelt to scratch his tummy, her hair falling across her flushed face, her stomach churning weakly.

'You were looking for me? But why? We—we'd said—goodbye to each other.'

'We said a great deal,' Angelo returned abruptly. 'But I am not sure how much of it was true.'

'Well, I know the truth now.' She did not look at him, concentrating fiercely on Poco.

'If you are speaking of the letter I sent you,' he said harshly. 'I wrote it because I was hurt and angry. I regretted it at once and tried to prevent it being delivered, but I was too late. And by the time I was able to return to Porto Vecchio, you had disappeared.'

'What possible right had you to be hurt and angry?' She did look up then, her eyes accusing. 'Or are you going to deny that you went back to Rome because of my cousin Silvia?'

'I deny nothing. I answered a cry for help from my grandmother.' Angelo strolled forward. 'Silvia had appeared at Nonna Cosima's house in hysterics, screaming that I had destroyed her marriage and that honour demanded I should offer the protection of my name to her and the child she was expecting by me.' He paused, smiling faintly. 'It was something of an emergency, you understand. I had to go.'

Ellie gasped. 'You find it amusing?'

'Most absurdities are laughable, *mia cara.*'

Her voice shook. 'And poor Ernesto's broken heart—his humiliation at knowing his wife is having another man's baby—that's also a joke?'

'Ernesto,' he said, 'knows no such thing, and I doubt he would care anyway. He ended the marriage himself, Elena *mia*, by leaving your cousin very publicly for his secretary, Renata Carlone. They have been lovers for some time and I understand that when he has obtained his freedom, they will be married. I fear Silvia is the one to be left humiliated.'

'But he adored her,' Ellie protested. 'He was desperately jealous of every other man who came near her.'

'Once, perhaps,' Angelo said grimly. 'But his passion for her now, like the baby she claimed to be expecting, exists only in her imagination.'

Ellie took a breath. 'You mean—she's not pregnant?'

'Not by me. Nor by anyone else,' he said tersely. 'Once I confronted her, demanding that she should submit to the usual tests, and warning her that I would insist on DNA evidence in due course, she became first evasive—then sullen—before finally admitting she could not be sure of her condition. In other words, she was lying.'

'But she came to see me,' Ellie protested. 'She—she told me that you were still her lover, and thrilled about the baby, which was why you needed the quickest possible divorce or annulment.'

'And you believed her?' Angelo's tone was incredulous. 'In spite of everything she has done? And in spite of everything that you and I have been to each other?' He closed his eyes. '*Santa Madonna*, how is it possible?'

'But she knew—about us,' Ellie insisted desperately. 'She knew everything. She said you'd simply been doing what was necessary, for her sake, to persuade me to agree to whatever you wanted.'

'And so I did, *carissima*,' he said quietly. 'But for my own sake, not hers.'

Ellie lifted Poco into her arms. Held him like a shield. 'But how could she know what had happened between us unless you told her?'

'Quite easily, *mia bella*. I have suspected for a while that I was being watched, and at Porto Vecchio, I became certain of it. There was a woman staying at the hotel who somehow contrived to be on the beach—at the *trattoria*—everywhere that we went.

'I spoke to Ernesto and he told me he had found fees for a private detective agency on Silvia's credit card, and thought wrongly that he was their target.'

He shrugged a shoulder. 'Clearly, she was hoping for evidence of my infidelity in order to make trouble between us. Instead, she discovered only that I was having an affair with my own wife.'

Ellie looked away. She said in a low voice, 'Or pretending to do so.' She rallied. 'But you still wanted her. I—I saw you together at that reception, remember. Saw the way she looked at you and how you smiled back at her.'

'Body language can be deceptive, *carissima*,' he said. 'To an onlooker, it may well have appeared a pleasant conversation. But what a pity you cannot read lips instead, or you would have known that I was telling her with great frankness that she was wasting her time. That it was over between us long ago. That she would never have any place in my life, and I wished her not to approach me again.'

'Oh.' Ellie swallowed, trying to steady the turmoil in her mind. 'Where is Silvia now?'

'She has thrown herself on the mercy of your godmother,' he said drily. 'But I understand Prince Damiano is already tired of scenes and tantrums and has delivered an ultimatum, ordering her to leave.'

She said bitterly, 'And the Prince's orders are invariably obeyed, as I know to my cost.'

'Do you mean that?' he asked gently. Another long stride brought him dangerously close. 'Has our life together always been so unbearable? Can you look into my eyes and tell me so?'

She didn't dare look at him at all. She said huskily, 'Don't—please. You never wanted to marry me. We both know that. Why didn't you just let me go? Why did you come after me?'

Angelo was silent for a moment. 'I must be completely honest, *carissima*. And the truth is that I did not wish to be married at all. I resented the family pressure being exerted upon me to—do my duty, and furiously angered by the trick Silvia played on us both.

'But once you became my wife, Elena, things changed. *I* changed. Vostranto was a house I loved, but, with you as its mistress, it became more. It turned into a home—a place that I cherished and was glad to return to, even though you treated me like a stranger each time I did so,' he added wryly. 'Keeping always at a distance and barely speaking to me.'

He sighed abruptly. 'I told myself I should find comfort elsewhere. I even went looking, but still spent my nights alone.

'When you finally agreed to share your bed with me, I accepted your terms because, in my arrogance, I believed I could eventually persuade you to surrender—to enjoy being in my arms.

'Only it never happened. Each time we lay together, you shrank from me. Withheld the slightest response, even a kind word.

'I was once told some nonsense about a woman's body rejecting the seed of a man she did not truly love, but I began to wonder if it could be true. If you hated me too much to make a baby with me. And I realised the hell our marriage must have become for you.

'And when you ran away rather than submit to me again, I knew I could not go on torturing you like this.

'So I followed you to Porto Vecchio to tell you not to be

afraid any more. That I would not make you more unhappy than you already were by persisting with our marriage.

'But, seeing you—watching you on the beach that first morning, I saw a girl I did not recognise. No longer withdrawn and reticent, but someone who sang and laughed and danced in the waves. Someone I longed to know in every way.

'And I began to wonder if we had met as strangers in a distant place, without outside interference, whether things could have been different between us. If we might have fallen in love and found we wanted to spend the rest of our lives together.

'I decided there and then that I had to know. That I must discover if it would ever be possible to win you for my own, so, perhaps mistakenly, I became Luca, and courted you as my Helen.'

He took Poco from her arms and set him gently on the ground. Took her hands and drew her down beside him on the bench.

'I bought Casa Bianca, *mi amore*, because it was there I experienced the only true happiness of my life. Where I learned the enchantment of making love to the woman I loved. Of enjoying life's simplicities in her company. Of becoming a real husband to my adorable wife, the other half of myself.

'I believed what we had created there would go with us when we became Angelo and Elena once more, as, eventually, we would have to do. Instead, I faced the worst rejection of all and realised I had failed. That you *might* have learned to welcome my lovemaking but you did not want my love, because your freedom was far more important to you than any future we might have together. As if we had been playing some game, which had now ended.'

She tried to say his name and he put a quiet finger on her trembling lips.

'One moment more, *carissima*. I returned to Rome feeling defeated—empty. In a way, I welcomed your cousin's ludicrous intervention because it gave me a focus for my anger, and made me realise that I too would go to any lengths to get you back, even when I found you had run away again, and all hope seemed lost.'

He took a deep breath, his hands tightening on hers.

'And this is why I have come to find you, Elena *mia*. To ask you to come back to me and learn, if you can, to love me as I love you. To be my wife forever.

'I told Mother Felicitas that I had come to take you home, and even if you send me away again, *mia bella*, I shall not give up. Ah, my sweet one, will you not even look at me?'

She met his gaze, saw the uncertainty that haunted its tenderness and hunger.

She said quietly, 'Don't you see—I had to keep you a stranger. I thought it was the only way I could avoid a broken heart. I knew Silvia still wanted you—was obsessed with becoming your Contessa. She came to Vostranto and told me so. Told me she could get you back, and I believed her.'

She took an uneven breath. 'All my life, it seemed, I'd been the shadow to her sun, and I told myself that would never change. That I'd never be more than the girl who'd been forced on you, and, therefore, keeping you at a distance would be my only salvation. Because I couldn't bear to be touched, knowing you wished I was someone else. And I was scared that one night I would let you see how I really felt, and that you might laugh at me or, even worse, pity me.

'Then—seeing you with her that night at the reception, I realised this half-life I was living had become impossible. That if you wanted Silvia in return, I'd have to go away—somewhere I wouldn't have to see it. Wouldn't wonder every moment of the day and night if you were with her. Imagining you…'

Her voice broke. Angelo took her in his arms and held her close, his cheek against her hair, his voice murmuring words she had never believed she would hear.

'So,' he said at last, using his handkerchief carefully to blot away the tears she'd been unable to contain. 'I cannot kiss you as I wish to do, *mia bella*, because once I start, I will not be able to stop and I have no wish to offend Mother Felicitas who has kept you safe for me.'

He ran a finger down the curve of her cheek. 'You will come back with me and our dog to Vostranto and make it a home again instead of an empty shell?'

'Our dog?' Ellie glanced down at Poco, peacefully snoring under the bench, and gave an involuntary giggle. 'My God, you mean you've kidnapped him again?'

'No, no, *carissima*. The Signora is going to live with her son, whose wife does not care for animals, so she offered me Poco—as a wedding present. It seemed a good omen.'

He paused. 'Is it, Elena? Will you now say the words I most want to hear, and tell me that you love me? That we will be man and wife forever?'

Ellie said softly and simply, 'I love you, Angelo, with all my heart. I always did and I always will.'

She smiled into his eyes, all shadows fled. 'What is more, my darling, I can prove it.'

She took his hands in hers, kissed them gently, then carried them to her body, holding them to the place that sheltered his child, her shining face telling him all he needed to know.

* * * * *

Harlequin *Presents*

Coming Next Month

from **Harlequin Presents®**. Available September 27, 2011.

Coming Next Month

from **Harlequin Presents® EXTRA**. Available October 11, 2011.

HPECNM0911

Visit www.HarlequinInsideRomance.com
for more information on upcoming titles!

REQUEST YOUR FREE BOOKS!

◆ Harlequin *Presents*~

PASSION GUARANTEED SEDUCTION

2 FREE NOVELS PLUS
2 FREE GIFTS!

YES! Please send me 2 FREE Harlequin Presents® novels and my 2 FREE gifts (gifts are worth about $10). After receiving them, if I don't wish to receive any more books, I can return the shipping statement marked "cancel." If I don't cancel, I will receive 6 brand-new novels every month and be billed just $4.30 per book in the U.S. or $4.99 per book in Canada. That's a saving of at least 14% off the cover price! It's quite a bargain! Shipping and handling is just 50¢ per book in the U.S. and 75¢ per book in Canada.* I understand that accepting the 2 free books and gifts places me under no obligation to buy anything. I can always return a shipment and cancel at any time. Even if I never buy another book, the two free books and gifts are mine to keep forever.

106/306 HDN FERQ

Name _____ (PLEASE PRINT) _____

Address _____ Apt. # _____

City _____ State/Prov. _____ Zip/Postal Code _____

Signature (if under 18, a parent or guardian must sign) _____

Mail to the **Reader Service:**
IN U.S.A.: P.O. Box 1867, Buffalo, NY 14240-1867
IN CANADA: P.O. Box 609, Fort Erie, Ontario L2A 5X3

Not valid for current subscribers to Harlequin Presents books.

**Are you a current subscriber to Harlequin Presents books
and want to receive the larger-print edition?
Call 1-800-873-8635 or visit www.ReaderService.com.**

* Terms and prices subject to change without notice. Prices do not include applicable taxes. Sales tax applicable in N.Y. Canadian residents will be charged applicable taxes. Offer not valid in Quebec. This offer is limited to one order per household. All orders subject to credit approval. Credit or debit balances in a customer's account(s) may be offset by any other outstanding balance owed by or to the customer. Please allow 4 to 6 weeks for delivery. Offer available while quantities last.

Your Privacy—The Reader Service is committed to protecting your privacy. Our Privacy Policy is available online at www.ReaderService.com or upon request from the Reader Service.

We make a portion of our mailing list available to reputable third parties that offer products we believe may interest you. If you prefer that we not exchange your name with third parties, or if you wish to clarify or modify your communication preferences, please visit us at www.ReaderService.com/consumerschoice or write to us at Reader Service Preference Service, P.O. Box 9062, Buffalo, NY 14269. Include your complete name and address.

HPI1B

*Harlequin Romantic Suspense presents the latest book
in the scorching new* KELLEY LEGACY *miniseries
from best-loved veteran series author Carla Cassidy*

*Scandal is the name of the game as the Kelley family fights
to preserve their legacy, their hearts…and their lives.*

Read on for an excerpt from the fourth title
RANCHER UNDER COVER

*Available October 2011
from Harlequin Romantic Suspense*

"**W**ould you like a drink?" Caitlin asked as she walked
to the minibar in the corner of the room. She felt as if she
needed to chug a beer or two for courage.

"No, thanks. I'm not much of a drinking man," he
replied.

She raised an eyebrow and looked at him curiously as she
poured herself a glass of wine. "A ranch hand who doesn't
enjoy a drink? I think maybe that's a first."

He smiled easily. "There was a six-month period in my
life when I drank too much. I pulled myself out of the bottom of a bottle a little over seven years ago and I've never
looked back."

"That's admirable, to know you have a problem and then
fix it."

Those broad shoulders of his moved up and down in
an easy shrug. "I don't know how admirable it was, all I
knew at the time was that I had a choice to make between
living and dying and I decided living was definitely more
appealing."

She wanted to ask him what had happened preceding
that six-month period that had plunged him into the bottom

of the bottle, but she didn't want to know too much about him. Personal information might produce a false sense of intimacy that she didn't need, didn't want in her life.

"Please, sit down," she said, and gestured him to the table. She had never felt so on edge, so awkward in her life.

"After you," he replied.

She was aware of his gaze intensely focused on her as she rounded the table and sat in the chair, and she wanted to tell him to stop looking at her as if she were a delectable dessert he intended to savor later.

Watch Caitlin and Rhett's sensual saga unfold amidst the shocking, ripped-from-the-headlines drama of the Kelley Legacy miniseries in

RANCHER UNDER COVER

Available October 2011 only from Harlequin Romantic Suspense, wherever books are sold.

Copyright © 2011 by Carla Cassidy

HRSEXP1011

SPECIAL EDITION

Life, Love and Family

Look for
NEW YORK TIMES AND *USA TODAY*
BESTSELLING AUTHOR

KATHLEEN EAGLE

in October!

Recently released and wounded war vet
Cal Cougar is determined to start his recovery—
inside and out. There's no better place than the
Double D Ranch to begin the journey.
Cal discovers firsthand how extraordinary the
ranch really is when he meets a struggling single
mom and her very special child.

ONE BRAVE COWBOY,
available September 27 wherever books are sold!

www.Harlequin.com

SE656257KE

Harlequin

INTRIGUE

FAN-FAVORITE AUTHOR

DEBRA WEBB

BRINGS YOU MORE OF THE BESTSELLING INTRIGUE MINISERIES

Casey Manning is on a top secret mission to track down
a man who has been watching the Colby agency
for months. But when she is forced to work with
handsome Levi Stark, who just happens to work for a
rival agency, will the tension between them get in
the way of solving this top secret mission…or will it
bring them closer together?

CLASSIFIED

Available October 2011 from Harlequin Intrigue

Available wherever books are sold.

www.Harlequin.com

HI69574